Brewster McCabe
Ace Private Eye

by Robb Zerr

ISBN-13: 978-0692471036
ISBN-10: 0692471030

Designed by CommuniCreations, Inc.

Printed in the United States of America

Other Books by the Author:

Memoirs of a Buccaneer: 30 Years Before the Mast
RobZerrvations – Vol. 1

Dedicated to my mom, Donna, who loved a good mystery, including the one she called her son. She continually encouraged me to explore a world that existed only in my head and to celebrate my creativity and imagination, not fear it or apologize for it.

Contents

Chapter 1

The night was balmy and so was I. After all, it had been a long time since my last case: it was bourbon I think.

Here I sat, slowly surveying my office. It was filled with the memories of 10 years of sweat, tears and close calls in the private eye biz. To my right: a four-drawer file cabinet -- its drawers contorted with age. In it were the files of the cases I had solved. The other three drawers were empty.

To the left of the cabinet stood the water cooler. In an age of bottled water, no one had taken a drink from it in years but I kept it around for company. The occasional gurgle of a bubble rising to its crusty surface has been a steadfast companion over the years.

The rest of the room was done up in a typical private eye decor with just a touch of intrigue to accent the peeling walls.

The rhythm of the dull gray, monochromatic tone of the room was interrupted only by the frosted glass door.

The name on the window had faded almost as much as my memory but it was still legible, even in the faint light cast by an unpaid power bill.

It said:

Brewster McCabe: Ace Private Eye

"Available for murders, espionage, international intrigue and occasional weddings"

That was me, Brewster McCabe. A somewhat middle-aged man whose closest friend was a Redhawk .41 strapped to his shoulder. A man who had dedicated his entire life to filling other men with bullets so he could bring those who were left to justice.

But those years of triumph over the perennial forces of evil were seemingly drawing to a close for me. Private eyes were a dying breed – literally. Now, only the careful and the cowardly remained. How the moral fiber of this once proud pro...

But enough of this bellyaching. Booze tends to cause one to look back at his depressing past rather than his bleak future – a future which...

Suddenly there was a knock at the door. Each rap echoed endlessly through the sparsely furnished office.

At last, a client has come seeking help with a case. Maybe it was murder or blackmail or...

My internal monologue trailed off as the silhouette of a man appeared through a crack in the doorway. The light from the hall made it impossible to see who it was.

Knowing that the perp could be looking for some trouble and not being in the mood to accommodate him, I dove for cover, pulling my Redhawk from its holster as I fell prostrate on the floor behind my desk.

"Freeze sucker!" I yelled. "Up against the wall or have a lead buffet for lunch."

It wasn't a difficult decision.

The intruder inched the door open, moving slowly through the crack. He spread-eagled himself against the wall as instructed.

I carefully made my way over to the shadowy stranger so I could shake him down.

"Don't try any funny stuff. I've got one hand doing the frisking and the other's holding my rod."

He let go a giggle, until I jammed my gun into his rib cage.

A quick pat down confirmed my suspicions that he was packing a piece. He'd better be. He was my friend and apprentice, Lionel Finchley.

"So, if it isn't Lionel Finchley!" I said. "Apprentice Private Eye in the flesh."

"How are ya, chief? You're getting faster on the draw, even at your age."

"Instincts my dear boy. A talent you'll acquire as time goes on. You'll learn to handle yourself again in unfamiliar situations as you gain confidence."

Finchley and I had been friends since childhood. Until three years ago, he had been a first rate detective in South Chicago. One day a client literally spilled his guts in Finch's office; the sordid by-product of a shotgun blast that had ripped through the door.

Now it was up to me to put the pieces of his life back together once more. I had to refill that empty shell of a man and load him back into the barrel of life. I had to restore the spirit, drive and fear of starvation that are the hallmark of a first-rate dick.

But first there was a more pressing task at hand. New life had to be pumped into my business. I had to get a case soon or die trying.

The phone cut short my thoughts of eventual doom. I picked up the receiver. I spoke.

"Brewster McCabe, here. Ace Private Eye. No case too small -- no fee too big."

A woman's voice ended the pregnant pause of the unknown at the other end of the line before it gave birth.

"Is that you, Brewster?" she asked.

It was my mother.

My mother. It seems like only yesterday that I last saw her. Come to think of it, it was only yesterday. What a woman. Strong willed, domineering, authoritative, manipulative. They really broke the mold when they made mom and the world was better off for it.

The sound of her gruff voice jolted me back into the real world.

"Sonny, I just called to see if you've met anyone special yet. You know, a future ex-wife?"

It wasn't the first time my mother had asked this question. When in hot pursuit of the latest scuttlebutt, she was about as subtle as a blackjack to the back of the head. She taught me everything I know.

But unlike her, I get paid to invade the privacy of other people's lives. It's that kind of business you know. Nothing is sacred when it comes to destroying other people's lives and reputations for money. A good private eye can't have strong morals and a large bank account too. He had to choose one or the other. I have yet to decide.

"No mom," I replied after an unusually long pause to subconsciously validate the importance of my chosen profession. "I haven't found me a dame yet but it's still early. For cryin' out loud mom, I'm only in my 30's."

My mother was unusually understanding for a change.

"That's fine with me son. After all, I'm only your mother. You can throw your life away any way you please. Die a lonely man – break your poor mother's heart – who am I to tell you how to run your life? The life I gave you."

No matter how good or how bad things got in my life I could always count on mom to keep things in perspective for me. How? By consoling me in my hour of need? By offering some timely advice?

Heavens no. Not my mother. She relied upon that time honored maternal gift from God: GUILT! That invisible mother-son tie which can't be cut, but which can be easily reeled in whenever good old mom was in the mood.

But enough of this. It was time to finally take a stand. My mother could no longer be allowed to rule my life through these endless guilt trips. It was time to set her straight. Time to take a stand for what I thought was right. To stop straddling the fence of maturity and cross over to the side of manhood…

"Mom," I said with renewed resolve. "I'm really sorry but I must have lost my head. Yes… Yes… O.K. See you soon. Love you too, mom."

She hung up. The silence at the other end of the line was deafening. Guilt, that emotional umbilical cord of life, had won another round of tug-o'-war.

I returned the receiver to the phone on the desk.

Finchley put his hand on my shoulder. Men always seem to resort to this awkward attempt to reach out to their male counterparts. It made them feel better somehow – this display of concern. Not me. It made me feel cheap. Like a two-bit hooker who made change. I thrust Finch's arm from its awkward resting place.

"Don't worry boss," he said trying to console me. "Your mother won't be around forever. Someday she'll just drop dead or somethin'."

Finchley always knew the right thing to say to cheer me up.

"Thanks Finch, ol' pal. I don't know what I'd do without you." The thought intrigued me though.

Chapter 2

Here I was growing older by the sentence and I still had no business. I thought to myself: What is a private eye without a case? Or a six-pack at the very least?

I reached for my trench coat. True, it was a P.I. stereotype. But my life was a stereotype. I was lost in a mental fog and I owned a London Fog. Hmm!

"C'mon Finchley," I said. "Let's go."

"Where are we going McCabe? To find a case?"

"Yes. But first we'll grab a bite to eat."

The life of a private eye is a transitional one at best. But we dicks are used to doing the dance of death with the Grim Reaper all the time. Especially during lunch. Especially at Dirk's Diner.

Owner Dirk was long gone. He had moved on to greener pastures. Or was that he was planted in greener pastures? No matter. At least he didn't have to eat the diner's food anymore.

Dirk's customers are still giving 2:1 odds it was the food that killed him. I think it was the meat cleaver the police found in his back. Call it a hunch. Homicide said it was self-inflicted. I say it was revenge.

Food poisoning can do that to a person. Somewhere between the gut wrenching cramps and the vomiting, a customer loses his sense of humor. And Dirk lost his life as a result. It was no laughing matter.

Dirk's waitress, Dinah, took over the diner business after Dirk died. Dinah had been in the food business since the day she was born. And some of the food she served must have entered this world with her. To say her cooking was disgusting would be too kind.

But she had that way about her. Sharp-tongued, salty, muscular. She reminded all of us of our mothers. We called her "Mom." She called everybody "Sport."

No one has ever quite figured out who Sport was. He may have been her husband. He may have been her dog. But it didn't really matter. What did matter was that she had the ugliest tattoo on her arm. And whenever she flexed it, it would . . .

But I'm digressing. The thought of eating one of Dinah's lunches had a way of making one digress. It also had a way of making one extremely sick.

The alternative was even less appealing. Hunger was a strange bedfellow and I didn't want to roll over in the morning and look it straight in the eye. I've known that empty feeling. Rolling over and not knowing what her name was. At times like that I'm reminded of a liner note on an old Jimmy Buffett album: *The night wrote a check the morning couldn't cash.*

Man, I've bounced a lot of checks in my time . . .

But none of this had anything to do with the quandary my stomach was in at the moment. I've heard others talk about being adventurous eaters. At Dirk's though, eating was the adventure.

So here I was with my lifelong pal trying to choose

the lesser of evils for lunch.

By now you're probably wondering why I eat at Dirk's when the food is so consistently lousy. It's a case of simple math: 38-24-36.

Her name was Lola and she was the prettiest thing this side of the Mississippi. I was madly in love with her. I was sure she wouldn't give me the time of day, let alone the time of my life. But she poured a mean cup of joe.

"Coffee, McCabe?" she asked.

"Yes please," I replied, my heart racing in anticipation as she moved her supple, pouty lips once again to speak.

"Cream? Sugar?"

Sugar! It was the first time Lola had called me that. How I've dreamed this day would come. It was difficult to hold back from embracing her fondly. Or was that fondling her embracingly?

But I acted coolly. I spoke deliberately, choosing just the right words to say to my beloved Lola.

"Cream."

What is it about a woman that can make a debonair, man-about-town like me so tongue-tied? What kind of spell can a woman cast that makes a man weak in the knees and stiff in the . . .

I can't help but wonder: "What's a nice girl like her doing in a place like this?"

Dirk's was filled with the flotsam and jetsam of the earth. Convicted serial killers out of the slammer on good behavior. Dealers, druggies, bar babes and the lowest form of life of all – door-to-door salesmen.

To the uninitiated, these door-to-door sellers were hard to tell apart from the dealers. But there are some stark differences.

Dealers shop at Brook's Brothers. Salesmen: The Bargain Basement.

Whenever I see one of these guys, I'm reminded of the advice my brother gave me as I contemplated my future in the working world. He said, "Brewster, don't worry about failing in any career. You can always be a salesman."

I can thank him for my limited success as a private eye because that bit of sage advice continues to terrorize me to this day.

Life as a salesman. Days, weeks, months filled with mindless chitchat, pitching the ol' hard sell to poor little old ladies and wearing polyester (ugh!).

Where in the hell do these guys find these suits?

After all, I remember standing alongside the rest of the fashion-conscious free world heralding the demise of polyester suits several years ago when the leisure suit fad finally died out.

Remember this apparel some people had the guts to call clothes? Back in the 70s you could always tell the "Polyester Princes" miles away because they gave the any open flame or candle a very wide berth.

I have no idea where salesmen continue to find these cheap suits. But I have a theory. They must all shop at the same place because they all seem to know one another. They even look like they enjoy recognizing one another from across a crowded room.

This is particularly true at a place like Dirk's. A salesman walks into the diner and 30 minutes later he finally exhausts his supply of business cards and off-color jokes accented with obscure punch lines.

I never would have made it selling metal detectors at Radio Shack.

Not that I'm making it as a detective. But at least I don't have to ooze all over people and smell like a cheap bottle of after-shave.

A cheap bottle of liquor, yes. But cheap after-shave? Never!

Well, almost never. Occasionally – in the line of duty mind you – I must dabble in the art of female seduction. Oh, I know what you're saying: "You dicks are all lady's men."

But that's not true. Some of us are just dicks, doin' the dance of death with the Reaper. But I must admit, there are dicks and then there are DICKS!

A poke to my arm wrested me from my waxing philosophic moment.

"What do you want, goddammit? Can't you see I was thinkin'?'"

"But boss, your lunch is getting cold. I thought you might like to eat it before it gets cold."

"Why thank you, Finchley. How observant of you. Your keen private eye instincts are as good as ever aren't they? Did you happen, by any chance, to notice what I ordered today? A Chef's Salad, Finch. It's supposed to be cold."

"Would you like me to ask the waiter to take it back

into the kitchen so they can warm it up for you?"

I was contemplating putting him out of my misery with a few slugs from my automatic when my darling Lola reappeared tableside.

"How is everything today, McCabe?"

"The food or the company?"

"Can I get anything else for you before I get off – work that is?"

It was an open-ended question begging to be answered. But I let it slide, knowing that I was on duty right now and my insatiable lust for money outweighed my insatiable lust for Lola. At least for the moment.

"Thanks Lo, but I think you're just fine . . . I mean we're just fine."

As she turned her assets toward me and walked away, I turned to gaze out the window. Life was passing me by at a hectic pace and I was stepping through it faster every year.

How could I let such a wonderful woman slip through my fingers? Was it because I was destined to die a lonely man? Was fate playing out the ultimate practical joke? Or was it Bubba, Lola's Neanderthal boyfriend who was a bouncer at the Pink Flamingo by night and a hit man for the Jamaican mob by day?

No, there would be no little Brewsters playing cops and robbers in the backyard. No crocheted shoulder holsters. No snub-nosed cap guns blazing away in the twilight of a warm summer's eve.

I was a loner for a reason. And someday I'll find out

what it is.

Only one other woman had ever gotten this close to my hardened heart. It was my high school sweetheart, Doris. We met at International Night in the school's cafeteria. She was selling Ojo de Dioses in the Spanish class booth when I first laid eyes on her. What a doll. We were inseparable from that point on – until she gave me mono.

That's Infectious Mononucleosis for those of you who are not in the medical profession. I suffered from the complications for months, married her and she suffered with me as a husband for the next five years. She finally bounced me out on my butt when she found that my hands, along with several other vital body parts, were in someone else's cookie jar.

All things considered though, it was an even trade. I've always believed in the "eye for an eye" philosophy. I'm sure she'll find somebody who's perfect for her someday. Like I should be the one to cast stones with my sad love life.

Oh sure. There have been others. An assortment of bimbos, floozies and airheads. Even a millionairess once. But a woman of substance is a rarity, especially one who can speak in polysyllabic terms and keep the lights on. A vocabulary that relies almost exclusively on *yeah, huh* and *ya' know* can wear thin pretty fast. Not that I'm an Einstein or anything but I do enjoy a complete sentence occasionally. Ya' know?

Of course, all of this introspection does little for the future of my private eye business. Or for my reputation.

"Let's go, Finch. I feel lucky. A case is going to come

our way soon. I can feel it in my bones."

We left the familiar red vinyl booths and velvet paintings of overweight dead singers lining the walls of Dirk's and stepped out onto the once bustling sidewalks of Seattle's Pioneer Square.

The Square is the oldest part of town, much of it pre-dating the Great Fire of 1889. It was also one of the rougher parts of the city.

A lot of people east of the Rockies think we're still fighting Indians in the Pacific Northwest. The truth is, they surrendered their bows and arrows to us years ago in exchange for a bottle of Thunderbird and a park bench in Pioneer Square.

My heart still aches every time I walk past them. A once proud nation of highly civilized people brought to their knees by a bunch of white men bent on stealing their land.

Californians aren't much different today. Selling their mediocre houses down south for a cool mil and picking up a sizeable estate in Washington for a fraction of that. Real estate values haven't been the same since. I think I know how the Indians must have felt.

My office was located in the core of the Square in a run-down brick building in desperate need of an earthquake to take it out of its misery. The elevator had gotten the shaft long ago – trapped between floors. And lucky me, my office was on the top floor.

Faced with no other options, Finchley and I huffed and puffed our way up the seemingly endless stairwell. Geez, it was a long way to the top. Every step announced our progress with a loud creak as our feet stopped briefly to say hello. At the top, we paused to catch our collective breaths. I made a vow right then and there never to have another office on the second floor.

The Seattle Times was waiting for me, heralding the latest scandals in banner headlines:

Luck o' the Irish Club urges cereal boycott: A Farewell to Charms

Attorney General serves Mayor Rice at council meeting

So typical of today's journalism. No wonder I chose the life of a snoop over the life of a stupe. God, journalists are a stupid lot – lulling themselves into believing all that crap about being objective when we all know they're printing whatever they want; blowing things out of proportion; ruining the lives of innocent people; taking an egocentric joyride on the troubled soul train of the oppressed.

And to think that in my younger days I wanted to be an investigative reporter. That was, until I found out some 300 journalists disappear each year worldwide without a trace. Result: instant career change.

Not that we dicks fair much better. But we do have one hell of an adventure in the meantime. And isn't that what's important? The adventure?

As Finchley and I entered the dank office I called home, a flashing light caught our attention. Now I know what you're thinking: the old flashing neon HOTEL sign just outside the window overlooking the street below.

You don't give me much credit do you? Thinking I'd resort to every literal stereotype possible to describe this ramshackle dump. Shows what you know. The sign burned out last October.

No, the light emanated from the most important innovation known to low-budget operations like mine: the answering machine.

Who needs a bitchy receptionist who has the audacity to request a paid vacation a year in advance – just to see her dying mother for the last time – when you can rely on one of these babies to do her work 24 hours a day, seven days a week.

I punched the PLAY button and waited impatiently for the whirring tape to come to a stop.

An electronic beep announced the arrival of the first message which now boomed through the sparse office, causing the folks manning the Pacifists International office next to me to bang violently on the wall while shouting, "Turn that crap down or we'll beat the shit out of you, you mother------!!"

The voice on the tape was a familiar one. A chill went down my spine. It was a dream come true.

"McCabe, I really need to see you tonight. I have a big problem, McCabe. A *really big* problem. And you're the only one who can help me out of the jam I'm in."

It was Lola.

Was she trying to butter me up or was she in a pickle? And if she was, just what was at stake? I desperately needed the bread but she could be just egging me on, trying to rub salt in the open wound of my heart. But her proposition was definitely food for thought.

"Meet me at the TNT in West Seattle," she said. "Eight p.m. sharp!"

"Well Finch, ol' pal. Lucky for her my calendar is open. I usually like to play hard to get."

Chapter 3

West Seattle is just a hop and a skip from Pioneer Square but it's a giant leap politically and culturally from the rest of the city. The word Seattle is just about all West Seattle and the rest of the city have in common.

I learned this the hard way when I moved there a few years ago from a three-room flat in the northern part of town. As most transient apartment dwellers do when they move into a new place, I immediately headed to the nearest social and economic hub to check things out.

I parallel-parked my rusting '73 Chevelle, the Green Monster as she is known, on California Avenue, the main drag through West Seattle. This area is known by locals as "The Junction." If you call it anything else those who live in the area will know you're not from here and yes, they will correct you.

These are the same people, mind you, who mounted a massive petition effort to secede from Seattle and become an independent city. The petition drive was a battle cry of freedom after a freighter piloted by a drunken captain rammed the West Seattle Bridge, jamming it in the open position. This made it extremely inconvenient for Californians to buy up houses for a song in West Seattle and then bitch about the neighborhood being so backward they don't even have a decent sushi bar or Beemer dealership to frequent.

But I digress. Anyway, my first foray into this alien world included a stop at the local drug store to buy one of the most basic substances found in a single male's food chain: beer. Beer is a very versatile liquid that in a pinch, 1) doubles for wine in exotic recipes, 2) serves as mousse and drain cleaner in one fell swoop, and 3) makes any overweight, over-aged, oversexed couch potato feel like he's Mel Gibson after a six pack or two.

As the cashier rang up the purchase, I dutifully filled out my personal check and handed it to her.

"Do you have a local address?" she asked with a slight tinge of impertinence.

"It's right there on the check," I replied with a forced smile.

"Sir, this is a North Seattle address. You might want to have a local address if you plan to be in West Seattle for any length of time."

After some haggling, a driver's license, two credit cards and the address of my first born, I completed my transaction.

That's what West Seattle's like. Independent and proud of it.

It was five to eight by the time I arrived at the TNT. I would have loved to order a double bourbon, but the TNT was a tavern, beer and wine only, and not much of a selection at that.

My old drinking pal, Dee, was tending the bar.

I ordered a Rainier on tap and he and I went through our traditional greetings.

"Hey Dee! Why do debutantes hate group sex?"

"Don't know, McCabe. Why do they hate group sex?"

"Because they can't stand to write all those thank you notes the next morning."

Nobody in the bar laughed. It's tough to muster a guffaw when your jaw has just dropped to the floor.

Unknown to me, Lola had stepped through the door, mid-punch line. Talk about being upstaged. She was not your average TNT customer.

Lola was every guy's dream, and perhaps every girl's dream, too. As she entered the tavern, her blond hair lit up an otherwise dark room, as did her gorgeous smile. She was tall in her heels and dressed in a short black dress that hugged every curve of her body. She should have had little yellow road signs dangling all about her: WARNING: CURVES AHEAD. That indispensable wardrobe staple, the little black dress, never looked better. Was it getting hot in here?

"Hi fellas!"

The dozen guys in the bar were quiet, unable to even pucker up a wolf whistle.

She sauntered over to the stool next to me, then leaned over to whisper in my ear.

"Follow me, McCabe. We need some privacy."

I followed her up the stairs, hypnotized by the sauntering, swaying form in front of me. My pulse raced. Alone at last with Lola. How could I be so lucky? Would I get lucky? Funny, guys always wonder if they'll get lucky: women already know.

We sat down at a corner table upstairs, overlooking

the rest of the bar below. Lola seemed a bit distracted; she carefully scanned the patrons in the bar while I scanned her. I couldn't take my eyes off her plunging neckline. Lola had the most strikingly large… sapphire pendant I had ever seen. Emerald cut encircled by 12-point diamonds. It was captivating.

"Nice bauble, Lo! Where'd you get a piece like that on a waitress' salary?"

"From a friend, McCabe. What can I say? Guys like to give me things. This is one of my favorites, though. I never go anywhere without it. Now, can we stop talking about sparklers and get down to business?"

"Sure," I replied, still staring at the stunning orb on her chest.

"Brew, look at me. I'm up here and I'm in big trouble. You're the only one I can turn to for help."

"Gee, Lo. Since the day I first laid eyes on you, I've dreamed of the day you would need me. But I kind of hoped you'd want me in a different way."

"Sorry to leave you with only a wet dream, but this is really serious shit. I think someone is trying to kill me."

Death was serious business all right. Especially when it involved the girl who could someday consent to become the mother of my children.

I know lots of people Lola could make stiff but who would want to stiff Lola, the love of my life, the girl who I adored?

"How do you know, Lo?"

"Nothing major. Just little things. Like, I loaned my friend Deirdre my car yesterday. She parked it down at

Southcenter, you know, the big mall. As she was
walking away, the frigging thing blew up –
smithereens. You could have put all the pieces in your
pocket."

"You own a Pinto? They do that you know."

"Shit no, McCabe. It was a bomb man. A flippin' pipe
bomb."

"That's not much to go on. They're even pipe
bombing environmentalists these days. Anything
substantial?"

"For Christ's sake. Of course. You think I'd bother
you over something so petty as a car bombing? What
do you think? I'm a sissy?

"I've been getting these goofy calls at night, ya'
know?" she continued. "Really weird calls. Like three
or four in the mornin', the phone rings off the hook.
Well, it CHIRPS! CHIRPS! actually. Ya' know, I just
hate those new-fangled electronic phones. I wish they'd
bring back those . . ."

"Stick to the story, Lo. What were these weird calls
like?"

"Not like any of the others I've ever gotten. Nobody
ever talked on the other end of the line – they just
chewed. And we're not talking minor snacks here.
We're talkin' major meals. Like someone was at a
King's Table Buffet and it was happy hour. Mass
grocery consumption, McCabe. Mass."

"That's pretty weird all right. Reminds me of a girl I
once knew. Boy, could she pack the groceries away."

"I'm not interested in your dating resume, McCabe."
I had committed a major male faux pas, bringing up

other women. Not that I was a Don Juan. More like Don Want. Wanting this woman or that. Always reaching for the brass ring and settling for pot metal instead. But even if you're a dip in the Dating World, you never want the woman of your dreams to know that. So you resort to that old male standby – you lie about the quality of women in your past. Raising or lowering the quality to suit the tides of the moment. Mine was at flood stage right now.

"Sorry, Lo. I'm just trying to get a piece, uh, a tidbit, of information that may prove useful to me in finding the perpetrator of these foul deeds."

"So you'll help me, McCabe? I haven't got much money so I'm not sure how I can repay you."

"I'm sure we can find some way, Lo. I may not be cheap but I am easy."

I left Lola at the TNT and took the Viaduct back to my office in the Square. Finchley was awaiting my return.

Before I could even get all the way through the door, he was already grilling me.

"You want some coffee, McCabe?"

"No thanks, Finch. Well??"

"Well, what?"

I was beginning to think Finchley's parents had taken one too many dips in the gene pool.

"Aren't you going to ask me about my encounter with Lola?"

"Oh, yeah. How was your date?"

"It wasn't a date, you dipstick. Lola's in deep trouble. Someone's trying to knock her off."

"I thought you were, Brew."

"I said, 'knock her off,' not 'knock her up.' What do you think I am, a necrophiliac?"

"What a coincidence. My first cousin on my mother's side twice removed was a necrophiliac. Every time he got a little cut, he'd bleed and bleed and bleed. Couldn't stop it."

"That's a hemophiliac, Finch. Not necro. *Hemo.*"

"No, that was my second cousin thrice removed from my father's side. As I recall, he and his boyfriend are living on Capitol Hill, just off Broadway."

"Not homo, hemo. Never mind. We have more important concerns. We have to help Lola. And fast."

Chapter 4

Sometimes fast is not nearly fast enough. A knock on the door the next morning confirmed this.

After rolling out of the sack, I groggily opened the door. A familiar face greeted me. It was not someone I wanted to see.

"Good morning, McCabe," he said in a no-nonsense tone. "May I come in for a moment?"

"Sure Detective, Grits, isn't it?"

"It's Grist, McCabe. Homicide Division. Seattle Police. Geez, you know damned well who I am. I need to ask you some questions."

We sat opposite one another on the couch. He reached into his pocket and pulled out a little black and white photo. Handing it to me he asked, "Have you seen this person lately?"

"Yeah, yesterday. She works at Dirk's."

"You mean *worked*. Lola Chase was found dead this morning. A jogger found her in the tall reeds by Duck Island. We're runnin' an autopsy right now."

My face must have registered a 9.9 on the shock meter. I broke out in a cold sweat, tears welling up in my eyes.

How could this happen? Who would have killed my

beloved Lola? Was it Bubba? A stalker perhaps? Or was it the Caloric Caller?

"What was your relationship to the deceased, McCabe?"

In my moment of Grist, grief –

Let's try that again. In my moment of grief, Grist showed an astonishing lack of sensitivity. He was callous and cold, just like I usually am when I'm investigating a murder.

But this was different. This was Lola.

"I knew her from the diner, Grist. She waited on me and Finchley all the time."

"And when exactly was the last time you saw her?"

"Yesterday afternoon at lunch. She was our waitress."

"Is that when you gave her this?"

He pulled one of my business cards out of his pocket. On the back she had scrawled the address to the TNT.

"Yeah? So what? Women are always asking me out. Something you probably know nothing about, Grist."

"Funny, McCabe. Look. I have a job to do here. You'd better keep that bloodhound nose of yours out of this case or I'll squash you like a road kill. Got it?"

"Got it Grits. Nice seein' ya again. Now get out."

"It's Grist, dammit, McCabe. Grist."

"I get the gist, Grist."

I slammed the door behind him and made my way over to the phone. I didn't like lying to the cops. Sooner or later they'd figure out I was the last one to see Lola alive when we at the TNT. There were too many witnesses.

I fumbled my way through dialing Finchley's number. It took forever for him to answer.

"Finch, I need you to meet me at the office in a half hour. Someone's iced Lola. And we're going to find out who it is if it's the last thing we ever do."

As I awaited Finchley's arrival downtown, I carefully went through the events of the last 24 hours. Every little word that was said, every nuance, every move. Over and over in my mind.

What was the motive? Who could or would have done such a thing? How did she die? Would anything have come of us if she hadn't?"

Like the blinding light from a nuclear detonation, the light from the hallway suddenly burst into the room as the door swung open. The current of electrons racing down the optic nerve and striking the retina, like bugs hitting a windshield, jolted my pupils, lulled into a dilated coma by the once blackened room. It was definitely a sight for sore eyes.

"Finch, is that you? How many times have I told you ..."

Silent, the shadowy figure moved through the doorway and over to the edge of my desk. Everything was a shadow, or at most a shade of monochromatic gray. The blimey bastard tried to blind me.

"Mister McCabe? Are you Brewster McCabe?" the mountainous shadowy hulk bellowed.

"Yeah, and just who the hell are you and why are you

in black and white?" I thought I'd ask at least one question I could answer myself.

"I'm Bubba Ebanks. Lola's boyfriend."

I fumbled around until I found the switch on my desk lamp. With a click, the light came on. Standing before me was the biggest creature I had ever seen outside a zoo. Bubba must have weighed in at 375 pounds and his silhouette was that of a VW Bug turned on end. He was a crowd even in an empty room.

I remember the day Lola first told me about the Incredible Bulk. She had gone dancing the night before with a friend down at the Pink Flamingo. Some Macho Texas Jerk thought he'd take Lola for a little spin on the dance floor. Only Lo had no interest in this Cowjoke. To make a long story short, ol' Bubba took on the chap and beat the crap out of him. It seemed like a hell of a battle at one point as Tex got on Bubba's back and commenced to ride him like a mechanical bull. The final buzzer never sounded but the bell did – right after Bubba threw Tex the length of the bar into the bell the bartender rings when someone buys a round. Cost Tex $300 in drinks, two broken ribs and a dislocated jaw.

Of course, Lola thought Bubba was her knight in shining armor. She threw herself in his arms and disappeared into those massive appendages for three days. Six Canadian Mounties and a sled team were finally sent in to find her.

They had been inseparable ever since. Lola and Bubba. At least up until last night.

"McCabe. It's all over. I've lost the only woman who ever looked deep enough inside to find the real me."

"So there *are* several of you in there. I had a feeling this couldn't be all one person."

"All kiddin' aside, McCabe. We were planning to get married later this year and start a family. I wanted nine kids. All boys."

"You mean, 'Tiny Bubbas, hear them whine, would make you feel happy, make you feel fine?'"

"Cut the Don Ho jokes, McCabe. One more crack out of you and I'm going to send some of my Jamaican friends down here to pull the hairs out of your head one at a time. From the inside. Got it?"

"Yup. Got it!"

"Now where was I? Oh yeah. Anyway, the cops have already hauled me in, wanting to know my whereabouts. They want an alibi, McCabe. A damned alibi."

"So what's the big deal?"

"I ain't got an alibi. At least one I can use. You see, me and the boys were doin', how should we say, a little business last night. You know, reconciling overdue accounts. If you get my drift."

He looked at me with the eyes of a child who had just shoved his sopping wet dog into a microwave to dry him off. Absolutely pathetic. Hardly the expression of a hardened killer who was just as likely to greet you on the street with a baseball bat as a handshake.

But he was right. Even if his buddies would vouch for him, the truth would leak out through the grapevine and Marvin Gaye would hear it, along with countless California Raisins, some whom even resembled Michael Jackson.

That would be it. Bubba would be locked up for Murder One. Endless days in the slammer. Hearing after hearing. Then the trial. Numerous appeals. A stay of execution. A last minute appeal. Then the last meal. A meal that could go on for days, knowing Bubba's bulk.

No, the taxpayers couldn't afford this trial, let alone the last meal.

My course was set, the wind to my back, full speed ahead. Somewhere over the horizon lay the Isle of Truth, where someone could finally tell me where I come up with all this strange imagery. Maybe they could even tell me who killed my beloved Lola.

"She's my beloved Lola, you sap," snapped Bubba. "And don't you forget it."

I've got to stop thinking out loud.

"Look McCabe. Think about what I told you today. I think I can trust you. You were always close to Lola."

Little did he know how close I wanted to be.

Just then, Finchley walked in, panting from the walk up the stairs.

Seeing him enter, Bubba rose from his chair and turned to leave. "Thanks for your time. I'm sure we'll be in touch."

As the door closed behind him, Finchley broke the tension that hung from the rafters of the room.

"Who, or more appropriately what, was that?"

"Lola's beau, Bubba."

"He's quite a guy, isn't he?"

"He's several guys. C'mon, we have work to do."

Our first stop: the Medical Examiner's office. Forensics wouldn't have a completed autopsy report until late tomorrow, but we had to look for clues on Lola's body.

If our luck was holding, Grist hadn't been there yet to put the kibosh on our involvement. We'd be able to sweet talk our way past the receptionist and have a look-see.

We quietly made our way through the halls, keeping an eagle eye peeled for the detective. Geez, he was a pain!

The Medical Examiner's office was at the end of a long passageway, lined with numbered doors. The place reminded me what it would be like to play *Let's Make A Deal* in the great beyond.

But Carroll Merrill or Jay weren't waiting behind any of these doors, unless of course they were laid out on a slab with a tag dangling from their toes. In my many years as a private eye, I'd seen some things that would make Stephen King's hair stand on end.

You'd think I'd be used to all this corpse stuff by now.

But it's something you never get used to, I guess. This wasn't some two-bit haunted house the local Rotary puts on during Halloween. This was an honest-to-goodness house of death.

Gives ya the willys. Or the Dougs at the very least.

At the end of the hallway was Exam Room #8B, the

final resting place of Lola according to the log sheet left on the counter of the receptionist station. The station was directly across from the room, but no one was manning the phones. The coroner's probably dorkin' her on some slab, I mused.

We invited ourselves into 8B. But as I reached for the doorknob, I hesitated a moment to collect my thoughts and prepare myself for the grisly task that was before me. Finally I entered, with Finchley hot on my heels.

The room was bathed in the bluish light of some x-rays still clipped to the light box on the wall. A single light dangled from the ceiling, directly over the deceased.

"Come on Finch," I whispered. "We have some work to do."

I made my way over to the slab and pulled back the sheet, my mind creating all sorts of horrible, twisted visions of how she looked as I did.

But as the bluish light cast an angelic glow upon Lola's face, all fears had vanished. She was as beautiful as ever. An angel in death as she was in life.

I quickly scanned her body for clues. This would have been a pleasurable task in other times, but she was slightly cold to the touch. Reminded me of my ex-wife. She was cold, too. So cold that every time she opened her mouth a light went on. But that's another subject and yes, a very cheap shot.

The coroner hadn't started the autopsy yet, so they hadn't marked an 'X' on her spot, yet. Still, I could readily see a few things didn't quite add up.

First, there wasn't a trace of skin under her

fingernails and no signs of any blows to the body.
There didn't appear to be any sign of a struggle. So she
either got blind-sided or she knew her assailant.

"Hey McCabe," Finchley whispered. "Lookee here."

He was holding Lola's hand. Undoubtedly, he had
found something.

At first, I thought it was her unusual ring, a tri-tone
job with interlocking bands. But I was soon proved
wrong.

"Nice manicure, huh?" he said, without looking up.
"Wonder where she gets her nails done?"

"Jesus! Why do I put up with you anyway?"

Before I could get a final answer to the question, a
disturbance in the hallway alerted us to the presence of
others in the morgue. A very familiar voice was
reaming Nurse Cratchett about the importance of
remaining at her station. Gadzooks, it was Grist, that
pain in the ass flatfoot.

"Finchley, we've got a big problem," I whispered.
"Grist is here and he's not a happy man. If he finds us
here, he'll make our lives miserable. Or worse, we
could be sent up the river."

"Why would he want to take us on a cruise, McCabe?
I thought he didn't like us."

I didn't have time to explain.

"Look, Finch. We have to figure out something fast or
we're busted for sure. If only . . ."

"I'm really sorry detective, but the recent budget cuts

have hurt us down here in the morgue," said Nurse Cratchett. "We're short staffed and I can only handle so many jobs at once. We had three people in here at the same time to identify loved ones, ya know! It seems like everybody needs some body sometime."

"Fine, nurse," replied Grist. "I can't overstress the importance of keeping access controlled, particularly to those cases still under police investigation. I don't need to impress upon you the grave and stiff consequences you could face if evidence is tampered with. We certainly don't want another Kariokis case, do we? Now, if I could have the medical examiner files on the body in 8B. I want to look it over myself."

"You know I can't do that, detective. The coroner hasn't started the examination yet and I have to follow proper procedures."

"Like the procedure where you were instructed not to leave your post? I'll put it this way to you: You don't tell and I won't tell. The chart please, Ms. Cratchett. Now!"

Grist turned and walked down the hall, looking at the initial report. Although the coroner had only performed a cursory exam, Grist knew from experience that the King County Examiner's office didn't exactly have a sterling reputation for thoroughness. His keen police instincts were working overtime right now, to the detriment of his sleep, appetite, and marriage. It was always this way, he mused. Once on a case, he would concentrate so hard on solving it that he couldn't think of anything else. This case was particularly perplexing. No obvious signs of a struggle or injury, no witnesses had stepped forward, and the only suspect was her boyfriend, Bubba, who didn't have an alibi but didn't have a clear motive either.

His preoccupation caused him to bump into a lab technician and nurse leaving 8B. After excusing himself for being so clumsy, Grist entered the room. "Hmm," he thought to himself, "That nurse needs an Epilady – bad!"

The lab coats and scrubs were a last minute improvisation, but it's worked many times before. When Grist mentioned the Nick Kariokis case, I recalled the story and the ruse that kept a local reporter from going to jail.

The reporter, Don McGaffin, had a feeling that a police shooting was a set up, and the only way he could prove it was to sneak into the wounded officer's room to examine his gunshot wounds. If his hunch was right, the officer who had murdered Kariokis would have powder burns on his hand and abdomen from a close range shot. Kariokis was 20 feet away in the alley when he supposedly shot the officer. So, McGaffin donned scrubs, grabbed a chart and strolled brazenly past the police guards and into the room, nodding to them as he entered in a most professional manner. Once there, he lifted the bandages and, voila!, telltale powder burns. The only way the officer could have received them was from close range, meaning the officer shot Kariokis in cold blood, then shot himself to make it look like it was self defense. Case closed.

It's funny how you remember moments like these when you need them most. Life is just one long learning opportunity and as long as you keep learning something every day, your life is worth living. In this

case, my love of a good story saved my ass. Thanks
Don for the ruse. It worked like a charm, even if
Finchley ended up getting electrolysis because he
thought he looked pretty good in a skirt. I worry about
him sometimes.

Well, let's look at the old scoreboard for a minute.
Beloved Lola was dead. Bubba was looking for an alibi.
Grist was looking for a suspect. I was looking for a
good time. And Finchley was looking for an A-line skirt
that wouldn't clash with his new thigh holster. I'd say
it was quite a case so far.

It was also time to regroup, so Finchley and I headed
back to Pioneer Square.

"Ya know, Finch, I just don't get it. In all my years of
cracking cases wide open, this one's got me stumped.
There are no obvious clues, no motive, and Grist is
being a real pain in the ass about this case. I'm used to
him being difficult, but why is he riding us so hard this
time?"

"Simple. PITA," Finchley replied. "P-I-T-A."

I shouldn't have swallowed the bait, but my curiosity
got the best of me.

"What the hell are you talking about, Finch?" There
was undoubtedly a party going on in his head that no
one else was attending.

"PITA," he said. "Grist is a PITA – a Pain In The
Ass!"

"Uh-huh. Finch, why don't you go get the mail."

As he left, I turned back to the case at hand. I

carefully reviewed what little I had to work with. Lola had been the target of a pipe bombing and harassing calls from someone with the munchies. She and Bubba were getting along fine, at least according to Bubba. Her body looked almost untouched – no telltale bruises, scratches – nothing at all that says a struggle ensued. People just don't give up the ghost easily. Time of death was somewhere between the time she left me – around 9:30 p.m. – and the next morning when the jogger found her in the reeds.

I decided to drive up to Green Lake, partly to retrace Lola's last moments and partly to try to feel closer to her.

Finchley returned to the office just as I stood to leave.

"Got the mail, McCabe. Hey, Ed McMahon said we may have already won $1 million. Isn't that somethin'?"

"Why don't you handle that for me, Finch. I'm sure he'll love to hear from you. Me? I'm going out for a bit. I'll check in later."

I headed north on Aurora, taking the 65th Street exit. Well, miracles of miracles: a parking spot right by the old Aqua Follies aquatic theater. I can't remember the last time a spot has been empty there. My luck must be changing.

It was a sunny, late summer afternoon, so I decided the walk would do me good. The spot where Lola was dumped was not that far but I figured I could blow a little steam off by taking the long way around. Besides, some of the roller babes in bikini tops make the journey a little more interesting.

Making my way to the crime scene was a lot more work than I thought it would be. True, it was only about two miles around the route I was taking, but I had to keep dodging bicyclists, joggers, rollerbladers, and worst of all, mothers with strollers.

If I had my way, all stroller rollers would be required to take a course in driving these things safely. I don't know how many times I've had to make my way through a sea of totally oblivious parents wafting hither, thither and yon, pushing a stroller. Blocking this aisle, hogging that row, hitting totally innocent pedestrians, who, yes, I'll admit, are sans child.

This is certainly true at Green Lake. Even though the path is divided so people on foot can walk on one side and people with wheels can take the other, no one seems to have a clue where they should be. Getting a workout at Green Lake has nothing to do with the distance traveled; it's gauged by the number of obstacles successfully traversed.

Finding the crime scene wasn't exactly difficult. The tape marked "Crime Scene, Do Not Cross" was a dead giveaway. But I never imagined the effect the crime scene would have on me.

Standing there, I was overcome by her presence. The aroma of Chanel No. 5 with just a hint of Gee, Your Hair Smells Terrific. The vision of her sweet, though sometimes crooked smile, her tousled long blond hair. The cute way she politely laughed at my awkward advances. Oh, the tragedy of it all.

I took a look around. Just as I thought, the police had been pretty thorough. Not so much as a single strand of human hair was left at the crime scene. As I walked away from the shore's edge, I felt a tear roll from the corner of my eye and down my cheek. Getting soft at my old age. Geez, I thought: "I'm losing my objectivity over this case." I had to get a clear head about it or I would endanger my own life and the lives of those around me.

I was obviously deep in thought. It wasn't until I arrived back at the lot that I realized that the Monster was no longer there. It was about a half a block down the road, going for a joy ride on a city tow truck.

I ran after my car, shouting to the tow truck driver to stop. But it was no use. She was gone. As I returned to the spot where I had parked only a short time earlier, Grist was waiting for me.

"Should watch how you park, McCabe," he said. "You crossed the line. Just like always. You really should learn how to stay between the lines. The city spends good money on painting them there. Unfortunately, crossing over the line is not only illegal, but today it'll get you impounded buddy-boy!"

"Thanks Grist for the tutorial," I said as I walked over. I wanted to punch his lights out, but I knew it would only prolong the agony of dealing with him and the boys down at the precinct.

"Let's take a little walk, shall we?"

"Thanks, Grist. But I still like women. Perhaps another time."

"If you want you car back, you'll walk. Coppice?"

As we started down the walk from whence I had just come, Grist reached into his pocket and pulled out a fistful of pistachios. We didn't say a word to one another for a long time. He just continued to shovel nuts into his mouth, spitting the red and white shells out on the sidewalk.

Finally, I could stand the silent treatment no more.

"That's littering, ya know."

"Thanks for the, now what was that – uh, tutorial, that's it, tutorial. But you seem to have missed an important point: I don't give a shit.

"I don't give a shit about littering and I don't give a shit about you and your panty-ass investigations. You're a small timer, McCabe. A know-nothing, do-nothing, two-bit dick. And I can squash you anytime I want. And do you know why, McCabe?"

"Because your mother was once a man?"

Grist turned on a dime, turned beat red, glared right through me, ready to burst at every seam. He wanted to tear me apart.

"No you little faggot! Because I'm a cop, that's why! We're a tight lipped, tight knit community of…"

"…Tight asses?" I couldn't resist finishing the thought for him.

"Look, McCabe. I've lost all my patience with you. Stop interfering with this investigation and stop pestering me. I'm a year away from my retirement and I don't need the likes of you messing with my pension. I will make sure, right down to my last breath, that you never see the light of day again. Got it?"

Without waiting for the answer, Grist turned and walked away.

As I stood there on the walk, I could feel the smug look on my face.

"Got him!" I thought to myself. "Got him goooood!"

Chapter 5

Grist slowed me down a bit with the impound trick, not to mention the $110 it cost me to get the Monster out of impound. It also set me back a couple of hours. But no matter. My next stop wasn't on the schedule, and by coincidence, was another questionable venture.

While waiting for my car, I called in a favor down at the DMV and ran a check on Lola's records. Her last listed address was just off 85th, a couple blocks away from the Baranof, where she waitressed at one point.

Her house wasn't hard to find. The police tape made it stand out among the others in the neighborhood. No doubt they'd already been through the place looking for evidence. As I drove slowly by, I didn't see any signs of life and there wasn't a patrol car in sight.

Parking out on the street would have drawn too much attention, so I pulled into the alley behind the house and brought the car to a halt in a set back. Stealthily, I made my way to the gate opening onto the backyard. Getting into the yard was the easy part. Getting into the house would be a little tougher.

After surveying the situation, I decided the cellar door was the best choice. I took the tool set out of my jacket and fumbled through the lock picks. Luckily, the lock was a cheapy Kwik Set and posed no problems. In like Flynn.

Except for one thing. The door in the cellar leading to the main floor was locked from the inside. One of those little consumer bolt latches, I thought to myself. Easy enough to muscle.

I stepped down a few steps to get a running start. I lowered my shoulder and charged upstairs, aiming all my might at the place where the little bolt was probably impeding my uninvited entry.

Unfortunately, I misjudged the situation ever so slightly. The inexpensive bolt was actually a large clasp, bolted to the frame with three-inch wallboard screws. And worse, the door opened into the cellar, not outward. When I hit the door, the frame split in half and the door, the frame and I sprawled across the kitchen floor. I'd be picking splinters out of my butt for a week.

But at least I was inside. I tried my best to return the door to its proper place, but with little luck. When the cops returned to the house, they'd know that someone had forced their way in. Talk about dumb luck and bad planning. I wiped everything down I thought I had touched so the cops would only find smudged prints. I then got down to business.

Lola's house was small, but immaculately kept. A place for everything and everything in its place. As I made my way down the hall to the bedroom, it didn't appear that the deed was done in the house. There wasn't any sign of a struggle or forced entry - except my own. The cops probably didn't find much here.

After the obligatory rifling of her lingerie drawers to unearth any perfumed letters she may have written to me, I returned to the living room. I was immediately drawn to the collection of photos on the mantle. There, arranged neatly before me, was Lola's short life. Her first communion. The high school prom. Cheerleading at a football game. Graduation. A family picnic at the lake.

I took the picnic photo from its frame and tucked it in my coat. I couldn't help myself. Lola looked great in her swimsuit. There was little else here for me. Except a stiff drink perhaps. Failing that, a beer.

I returned to the kitchen and stood for a moment in front of the fridge. Magnets held numerous mementos and supermarket receipts. I scanned the latest receipt: mac & cheese, Red Hook, Evian, a half pound of shrimp, yogurt, 2% milk, ravioli, spaghetti sauce. At least she had good taste. She didn't overlook a thing – including the Red Hook.

I popped the fridge and dove in for the micro brew. The fridge was empty. Not a leftover or bottled water in sight. Worse yet, no beer.

Strange. I stepped over to the counter and opened all the cupboards. It was Mother Hubbard all over. The cupboards were bare as well.

Now, how could someone go shopping the day before she was murdered and not have any food in the house? And if she ate all the food, wouldn't she be as big as the house? Hmm!

I returned to the Monster and drove back to Pioneer Square. This puzzle was getting more confusing by the minute. It was definitely one of the most difficult cases I had ever taken on. In fact, it was one of the few cases I had taken on.

I huffed and puffed my way back up the stairs to my office. With any luck, Finchley would still be there waiting for me.

"Finch, I never thought I'd say this, but I need your help."

He was on the sofa, out like a light.

"Finch?"

"Finchley!"

"Wake up dammit!!"

As I shook him, he finally regained his senses, what senses he had.

"Boss, it's you," he sputtered, grasping his head with both hands. "The last thing I remember was some footsteps behind me. Then WHAM! Everything went black."

"Drinking again, Finchley?"

"No, McCabe. Someone popped me one on the back of the head when my back was turned."

"Who'd knock you out? And why?"

"I guess they thought I was you, McCabe. Do you have some Tylenol or something?"

"No time for that, Finchley. I need your help. And I need it now. Remember, a truly great detective lives with pain."

"I think I'd settle for being mediocre right now."

"Congratulations. You've already peaked in your career then."

After giving in to his request for pain relievers, I went over the scene at Lola's house with Finchley. He listened intently, jotting down some notes as I dictated them.

"Ya know, if it wasn't for wanting a beer, I never would have stumbled onto the empty cupboards and fridge."

"Sounds like your house, McCabe. Remember Super Bowl weekend? All you had was three on the tree and some stale pretzels. It was about a '2' on the fun meter."

"Yeah, but I'm a guy. I'm not supposed to have fresh foods in the house. It's a guy thing, Finch. Something you'd know nothing about."

Wanting the conversation to take a less challenging turn, I pulled the picnic photo from my coat and showed it to Finchley. His jaw dropped halfway to the floor, obviously overcome by the stunning sight before his eyes.

"Quite a number, huh?" I said.

"Wow, McCabe! I can see what you mean. But who's the whale in the background holding the bucket of Col. Sanders? Bubba maybe?"

I snatched the picture from his hands.

"Good question. Why didn't I see this guy before? Oh, that's right, Lola in the swimsuit. C'mon! We've got work to do."

We made our way to Ballard to see an old friend at a local photo-finishing lab. The large young man in the photo may have been my first break. There he was, larger than life. Come to think of it, he was larger than just about everything else. In one hand, he held the bucket of chicken. In the other, a half rack of beer. But that's about all we could make out in the small print. Hopefully, Doug could enhance the photo a bit and help us identify the interloper.

"It's not going to be easy," Doug said, as he lowered his lupe. "The print's awfully grainy as it is and the subject, though large, is too far back in the picture. I can try to enhance it on the computer, but it's a long shot."

We walked back to the restoration department and waited patiently while Doug worked his magic on the photo.

"What's so important about this guy anyway, Brew? Is this another one of your wild ass goose chases you always seem to get me involved in? Let me guess. A man cheating on his wife. Or better yet, some dead beat who skipped out on a Jenny Craig bill."

I tried to play along, not wanting Doug to catch on to the murder angle.

"Yeah, that's it Doug. Ol' fatso skipped out on his bill. But it wasn't Jenny Craig. It was King's Table. Cost them a couple hundred bucks on Seafood Night."

We all chuckled as the scanner completed its conversion.

"So what is that thing, Doug?"

"It's a new Microtek sheet-fed scanner, McCabe. Pretty cool, huh? This baby cost a fortune but it can crank out images at 300 dpi, top of the line."

Not that top of the line though. The image was still

too fuzzy to make any kind of I.D.

"This is going to take a while, Brew. Why don't I give you and Finchley a call if I can get it any clearer. I think I'll try it the old fashion way – in the lab."

"Thanks, Doug. Appreciate the favor. Here's my number. Let me know if anything turns up."

By now, I was near total exhaustion. I had been on the trail for nearly two days without a wink of sleep. I decided it would be best if I got some shuteye.

After dropping Finchley off at the office, I headed back to the housienda for a much needed break.

Two days and we still hadn't gotten far. Now the sleep deprivation was beginning to cloud my judgment and dull my keen private eye insects, uh, instincts. See what I mean?

I sat down on the couch and slowly sank into a deep, deep. . . . .

"Why Lola, I just never knew you wanted me so." She forced me down on the couch and shed the last piece of clothing she had on.

"Make love to me Brewster. I want you. Take me."

She arched her back and fell back on the couch, which rocked ever so slightly because two books served as a surrogate leg on the right corner.

I moved to her, stroking her cascading mane of hair. I kissed her passionately, her smooth lips melting into mine.

And then it happened. Ever so faintly and then more pronounced…

RINGGGG! RINGGGG!

"Fire," she yelled, as she jumped to her feet.

"FIRE!," I yelled, sitting up in the bed. "FIRE!!!"

But there was no fire. And there was no Lola. It was the phone next to my bed. Somewhere on the border between consciousness and REM, the phone had entered one helluva dream. Again!

RINGGGG! RINGGGG!

I picked up the receiver and groggily greeted the caller.

"Brewster, it's me, Doug. I've got a better fix on the man in the photo. Can you come down here?"

I glanced at the clock. It was just after midnight.

"Why sure, Doug. I'll be there in the morning."

"No, Brew. Now! I don't think this can wait."

I really hate it when reality butts in on a really good dream. I'm sure it happens to everyone now and then. But with me, it always seems to happen when I'm just getting lucky with Lola.

I know what you're saying: "In your dreams."

But that's exactly right. In the nether world of sleep, you can be anything you want to be and get just about anything you want. It's free range in dream land, folks.

As for reality, I think it's overrated.

I made my way to the bathroom and ran a toothbrush

around my mouth. I'd forgotten to buy toothpaste again, but with any luck, there'd still be residue on the brush. There wasn't, so I opted for a couple of Tic Tacs and made a mental note to buy some toothpaste someday.

The Monster was ready as always. Faithful companion – though a bit homely. They just don't make them like this anymore. Thankfully.

I hopped behind the wheel and started the engine. It cranked over instantly. Oops, almost forgot to unplug it.

When I bought the Monster, it had traveled all the way from the great state of Montana. For some reason, people in Montana love to run a plug out the front of their car; for what reason I can't discern.

But being automotively challenged, I didn't want to risk ruining the car by forgetting to plug that plug in. So I always carried a 100-foot extension cord with me in the Monster to keep the plug plugged, just in case.

I rolled the cord up and tossed it into the back seat. Then it was off to the lab and the fat man.

I really hate driving after midnight. At this time of night, most of the cars around Seattle are filled with drunks. Now, that's not too bad when you're drunk, too. Then, everyone drives at the same impaired rate and you can actually convince yourself that those lines on the road are just guidelines for the less talented driver. Tanked up, you become Mario Andretti running on pure alcohol so you can dispense with following those sissy ass guides.

Ah, but when you're on the road sober and everyone

else is drunk, it's downright scary. Even for a seasoned pro like myself. After midnight, it's a cross between figure 8 racing and the demolition derby. And the Green Monster has had more than its share of street fights.

The lab was dark, except for a dim light up in a corner office. I tapped my car key on the glass door. I learned that trick from an old girlfriend. It makes the most obnoxious noise on the inside that no one can ignore. Try it sometime.

Doug bounded down the stairs and unlocked the door.

"This had better been worth it, Dougbo. I was deep in – "

"Another wet dream, McCabe?"

"No! You know that I grew out of that wet thing in my teens. Sort of."

Doug and I had been friends since high school. As seniors, we decided to run a mythical candidate for SBA Historian. Our creation, Larry Harwood, was a campaign manager's dream. He ran on the platform that "when the going gets tough, the tough eat prunes." Campaign banners heralded his vague attributes and we were well on our way to a big win.

That is, until his opponent started snooping into his background. Not to be outdone, we created bogus class schedules and transcripts. We even hired a guy to come in from another local high school and enroll officially as Larry Harwood.

I was the head of C.R.A.M.P., the Committee to Reelect A Mythical Person. Doug was in charge of F.A.R.T.S., the Forgery And Relocation of Transcripts System. We were nerds on a mission and it almost kept us from graduating.

From high school, we went our separate ways to some extent. Doug was in the dark most of high school, preferring to while away the hours in the photo lab instead of making the social scene. But he was good at what he did. And he loved to return to the underworld intrigue of his high school days occasionally by working with me on a case.

"So Doug, what do you have for me?" I asked, as we entered the dimly lit restoration department.

"It's downright exciting, Brew. Traditional lab techniques were a no-go. So I digitized the image into the Mac and tweaked the resolution and contrast in Photoshop. Then I enlarged the image back in the lab, isolated the subject and asked the computer to reconstruct the digitized image. And this is what I got."

Doug jiggled the computer mouse and the Opus screen saver gave way to the image of the fat man.

There he was, bigger than life. His wide grin was partially hidden on each side by his sagging jowls. His eyes were narrowly set, tucked behind a pair of wire rim glasses. His ears stuck almost straight out in an Alfalfa kind of way, his hair straight up in a crew cut.

"Get me a print of this, Doug. I'm not sure who this guy is, but he looks out of place in the photo. Just how many people passing by a picnic stop to pose for a family picture? Especially when it's not their family."

Chapter 6

So what was it about the guy in the photo that seemed so out of place? The fact that he was fatter than the rest of the gathered throng? Because he liked the Colonel's Original Recipe, even though no one else seems to these days? Hardly. It was the suit. In the middle of a hot summer day, one would have to wonder why a guy poses in a family snapshot in an off-white linen suit. Everyone else is in shorts and sandals and looking pretty toasty except for old saggy jowls.

It didn't take a keen detective like me to spot him, well, if it weren't for Lola in that smashing swimsuit. But the question remained, just who was he? Was Lola the target of some kind of stalker. . . the Caloric Caller perhaps? Or was the guy just hungry and passing through?

Without Lola to I.D. the guy, I had few leads. Unless the others in the photo could help me place him.

It was hard to wait until the morning. It seemed to take forever for the five hours to pass when morning checked in and it was socially acceptable to call. I turned off the boob tube as the snow of dead air became the strains of the Star Spangled Banner. I showered for a bit, made another mental note to buy toothpaste and Tic-Tacs and finally made it to the witching hour when I most likely wouldn't get chewed out for ringing someone's chimes.

I decided to first call Lola's uncle Cy, who Lola had introduced me to once at Dirk's. There was a slim chance he would know a face or two in the photo. Or if I was real lucky, he'd know who the Chicken junkie was.

"Cy, this is Brewster McCabe. I know we haven't spoken in a while, but…"

"Yes, you're a dick," came the reply. "And it's damned early for a dick to be calling me."

I wasn't certain if he really remembered me or was actually calling me a name. I chose to ignore his response.

"Yes, that's right I'm a private investigator."

"No, you're really a dick. Lola talked about you a time or two. Said you were something kind of special, she did. All she ever seemed to meet were the toughies, thugs and losers. But you were different to her. She really thought you were something."

The news stunned me. I retreated into silence for a moment, hid my shock and turned on my professional demeanor.

Before I could reply, Cy shattered the awkwardness of the moment. "She's gone you know. Dead!"

"Yes, Cy, I know. That's why I'm calling. And I can't begin to tell you how sorry I am that this tragedy occurred. My only hope now is to find the person who snuffed out her life and bring him to justice. But I need your help."

"Well, McCabe. In my book you are now, and will always be, a first class dick. Still, as much as I have disliked you from afar until now, I have no choice but to help you find the killer any way I can."

We met that afternoon at the Dog House, a 24-hour joint known for its rude waitresses, dog art and stiff drinks. The waitresses, with their vague indifference to even the regulars, were queerly endearing and somewhat legendary.

Perhaps my favorite part of the Dog House was the bar. It was festooned with photos of famous dogs, velvet paintings of dogs playing poker (I've never understood these) and the pianist belted out classic torch songs from days gone by.

It was my kind of place. Even in my youth, I realized that I belonged to another period in time. I was more at home in the era of extra dry Martinis, black Fedoras and smoky, dingy dives like Bob Murray's Dog House than a fancy wine bar. Back when it was still O.K. to call a chick a chick. And a five spot bought you a fine New York steak and a beer with change left over for a pack of Luckys.

Of course, that's what my mom told me about those days. I hadn't been born yet.

Too bad. I was almost too late to be a Boomer and I was too out of step with the 80s to be an Xer. I was in no man's land as far as a birthright. The only place I could call my own was being a private eye, which was not only no man's land, but a dead end.

I was on my second double when Cy finally arrived. I had almost given up on him. He consumed the room as he entered the bar, an energetic man in his early 80s, the cut of his jib that of an adventurer who had led a rough and tumble life most of us only dream about.

Before we lost touch, I had learned that Cy had been a shrimper in Key West in his younger days, smuggled contraband in Costa Rica, ran with the bulls in Pamplona, and ended his working days as a Merchant Marine in Seattle.

He would tell me stories of shrimping off Sand Key for Pink Golds, an elusive shrimp that only comes out at night in the Keys. And he would regale me with tales of drinking it up with Hemingway and Captain Tony well into the night as they spent their last dollar on a bad bet in a crooked cockfight.

Key West is a lot gayer than it used to be, and I'm not talking about happy. Now the town is largely segmented into the Breeder and Non-Breeder parts of town. In my youth, I too had dreamed of living in the Keys and did a short stint after high school aboard the Schooner WOLF, plying the sunset cruise tourista-trade for a couple years to earn enough to book passage home.

One night, a tourist puked on the back deck after drinking too much wine. That was it for me. I had washed my last puke-filled deck for low pay and headed back north to find other, more honest employment.

It was there that we found common ground, Cy's and my respective misadventures in the Conch Republic as young men.

Like many strangers brought together by a twist of time and space, we lost touch some years ago. Vague acquaintances that had briefly shared their lives over a shot or two, then took the next turn around the Rubik's Cube of life, never finding a solution that worked for them.

As I rose to greet him, the animosity we had on the phone seemed to melt away, at least temporarily.

"Hi, Cy. Thanks for comin'," I said. "I'll just cut to the chase here."

Cy ordered up a Cuba Libre from the snarky waitress who would more than likely make it a point to forget the lime.

"On the night before Lola died, she had contacted me about handling a case for her. She claimed she was being stalked by someone..."

"Spit it out McCabe," he said.

"...Someone with a big appetite for her. Like the nom, nom, nonstop vittles kind of appetite. I know that sounds strange, but she was getting phone calls at all hours. The caller wouldn't say anything. There was just heavy, deliberate breathing and some gnashing of teeth, as if the caller were trying to work his way through the thick gristle of a Chubby & Tubby steak."

"She never mentioned that to me," he said, finding that indeed his Cuba Libre was just a rum and Coke. "She did give me a jingle after the Pinto incident to let me know that she was O.K. But she never mentioned the calls. Are you sure it wasn't Bubba? Throwing a little scare into her to keep them together?"

"I don't think so. I ran into Bubba unexpectedly in my office shortly after the police picked up Lola's body at the lake. He was a mess. Sobbing uncontrollably about his loss and how he had an alibi, but it wouldn't check out because of its questionable legal interpretation."

"So, what's your take McCabe?" Cy said. "Do you have anything to go on?"

I recounted the events that had led up to the moment, including the visit to the morgue, Grist, breaking into Lola's house and the photo.

"Geez, McCabe. I think you've bent or broke every rule in the book. It's amazing that you're not sitting in the King County jail right now. Or dead. So how can I be of any help? Seems like you've already run into all the dead ends you could find on your own."

I fumbled in my pocket for a moment, then produced the enhanced print Doug had created. I handed it over to Cy.

After looking at it for a moment, he looked up and said, "So who's the fat guy in the suit?"

"I was hoping you would know, Cy. Lola had a picture of the picnic at her house – I think it was shot out at Lake Sammamish State Park. It looks like a family photo. Only this guy seemed out of place."

I produced the original photo and handed it over to him as well.

"Where did you get this McCabe?"

"It's the one from her house," I replied. "The police had gone over the place pretty thoroughly, but this photo seemed a bit out of place."

He studied it for a moment or two. Then he handed it back with my first break.

"It's family, but it's not family family," he replied.

"It's some of her coworkers from her days at Associated Grocers. Lola was an administrative assistant or something during their halcyon days. Then the bottom dropped out and the company cut back and Lola and half the IT department got pink slips when personal computers invaded Corporate America. This was from better times when the department had a company function or something at the park."

"Are you sure about this, Cy? Did Lola tell you about this?"

"Why sure, McCabe. This was taken a year or so before the AG massacre. I may be just an old fart, but I'm also a very nosy old fart. I was looking at the same photos during a visit with her and this one stuck out. I had to ask about it."

"Why this one Cy? Because of the guy in the suit?"

"No, McCabe. It was because of the woman with the bodacious humbungies trying to make their way to freedom from the crocheted bikini top."

I looked at the photo and sure enough, there was a very well endowed beauty in a white bikini standing next to Lola. If it hadn't been for the fat man in the back and Lola, of course, I may have noticed her earlier.

"I can see your point, Cy."

"You should see two, McCabe."

He did have a point about the points, that's for sure.

"But what about the guy in the suit, Cy? Do you know who he is?"

He took the photo back and glanced at it again.

"Beats me, McCabe. Seems a little out of place, I must

say. Especially since Associated Grocers was a business casual kind of place."

"Thanks Cy," I said. "I appreciate your help. I think I need to make a visit to some of Lola's old AG cohorts. They may have a better idea about who this guy is and what he was doing there that day."

I left the Dog House with a lead and the buzz of a double bourbon kicked into overdrive.

I jumped back into the Monster and returned to the TNT where my life had begun to unravel only a couple days before.

As I made my way across the West Seattle Bridge, I thought back to everything Cy had told me. It seemed strange somehow that Cy knew so much about his niece. But maybe that's what it's like in a close knit family.

I certainly had no idea what that was like, being from a close knit family.

I hadn't spoken to my brothers in years. I knew nothing about their lives or those of my nieces and nephews.

A deep divide, well, more of a chasm, developed when I chose the life I now lead. My brothers wanted me to go into the family business fixing televisions and radios.

Our father had left it to us after his untimely death. I think my father was a better repairman than he was a businessman. When he died, there were dozens of TVs still in the shop. None of them had customer names or work orders on them. They were all locked up in my dad's brain, which was now somewhere on the other side of eternity.

It was left to all of us to figure out whose set was whose and to not only find out what was wrong with them, but fix them as well and return them to their rightful owners.

That was simply not my forte. When I was created, the mechanical and electrical genes never found their partners in my DNA and I was dumb as a rock in these matters. So one day I broke the news that I was leaving it all to them to figure out.

They took it well. Rage let fly, fists followed closely behind and we haven't talked since. Except for my mother, I was an orphan. I guess that would mean I wasn't truly an orphan but you get my drift.

I parked around the corner from the tavern. As I entered, Connie, the day bartender, greeted me somewhat coolly. "What's wrong with her?" I wondered. Well, I meant more than usual.

She and I had had a fling several years ago before I found out she was a psycho. It took months to break things off. She just didn't want to get the message that we were finished. I think she finally got a clue after I had packed all her possessions into her car one evening and changed the locks on the apartment we were renting.

Luckily, she had found a new love so we were on speaking terms once again. Sort of.

"Well, if it ain't Brewster McCabe, ace private eye and general lowlife asshole. What you fixin' to have today? I have some lovely hemlock. Or how about a bit of arsenic? Maybe something a little more subtle – like having all your stuff packed into your car one night and the locks changed while you were on vacation?"

"Good to see you again, too, Connie. Sorry about the lock thing. But I'm glad you're not holding a grudge anymore."

"Little ol' me hold a grudge?" she shot back. "I'm just a sweet little ol' Texas girl, McCabe. And like all Texas girls, I'm a lady first, a vindictive bitch on wheels second."

She handed me a pint of beer, but not without it first overflowing onto the bar and into my lap. Point taken.

I returned upstairs to the same place Lola and I had sat on that fateful evening.

As I stared out over the abyss that separated the balcony from the bar below, my mind reeled with thoughts of the events that had transpired since then. I could almost see Lola's face still gazing at me from across the table, the radiant glow in her face now a bit more ashen, because, well, she was dead.

I made a few notes in my notebook about what Cy had told me. The coworkers at AG were my first hope of finding out who Grand Master Fat was in the photo. But since the big layoff, how would I be able to track any of them down?

Then it came to me with blinding clarity. I could just call Melissa, an old flame who had worked at Microsoft about the same time. She was now a millionairess after hitting it big in stock options after the company went public. She might have known some of these people as she had been embedded with Associated Grocers for almost a year as the company went from mainframe to PC.

I went back down to the main floor of the bar and reached for the payphone by the door. I called the last number I had for her in my address book. It had been a couple years since I last talked to Melissa, but with any luck she hadn't changed her number.

So you're probably asking right now: If Melissa was so rich, why wouldn't I just take up with her and get my mother off my back about the 'future ex-wife thing' and be set for life at the same time?

Boy, that's a good question.

She indeed had it all. A beautiful waterfront estate in Medina, enough money to keep me comfortable in the manner to which I'd like to become accustomed, a well connected circle of influential friends and an intellect that would keep my demanding mind stimulated forever.

She lacked just one thing though: Looks. There must be some kind of karmic balance in the procreation world. I have rarely met a woman of stunning looks who was also stunningly smart. Conversely, I've met a lot of homely women who were Einsteins and beauty queens who were dumb as rocks.

Shallow you say?

Don't get mad at me. I didn't make these cosmic rules of attraction up. I just observe them, jot them down and learn to live with them. That probably explains why I'm still a lonely, lonely man.

It's not that I want a smart woman in a real short skirt. But I'd like balance in the love of my life between beauty and brains. And this seems an impossible task.

And so, Melissa and I parted ways. She wanted more stability and breeding than I possessed and I wanted brains *and* beauty. It was a short-lived romance with lots of perks on my part. And I was the richer for it, literally, as she liked to shower me with extravagant gifts.

A voice answered the phone. "Ms. Owens' residence," she said in a slightly nasal tone. "How may I help you?"

"Is Melissa around? This is Brewster McCabe. We used to see each other socially."

"Ms. Owens is not available at the moment," she replied. "She is at her foundation function right now, setting up. May I take a message?"

Of course! I had totally spaced that today was the social event of the season. It had been in the papers just this morning: Melissa's fundraiser, an annual black tie affair at the Four Seasons that benefited the blind. Anyone who was anybody would be there."

"Can you tell me if there are any more tickets available to tonight's function? I'd like to help out Melissa's cause."

"You can probably still pick up singles at the foundation office. The foundation's number is (425) 226-6911."

I was in luck. They still had a couple tickets and after dropping $125 for one, I was set.

I returned to my palatial abode and quickly prepared for the evening's soiree. Cocktails were at seven so I had less than an hour to prepare and get downtown.

I opened my closet and pulled out my tux. Geez, I hoped the thing still fit me after all these years. The last time I had worn it was on my only Caribbean cruise through the Panama Canal. I got guilted into the cruise and relationship. The tux and the girlfriend both went into mothballs after we returned, still bickering as we said our goodbyes to one another. She and I, not me and the tux.

Thankfully it fit, but just barely. The cummerbund was a little snug around the old mid-section, which had expanded with grace since then as I traded in my six-pack for a pony keg.

I would have been in better shape if it weren't for those dinners out. I just never had much of a knack for cooking. Besides, as a single man about town it was tough to cook just the right amount. Recipes were for 4 to 6. For me, that would mean a week of leftovers. It was easier to eat out at the many greasy spoons around town. I wasn't much into fancy food either. Bacon and eggs for breakfast, a simple Club sandwich or Caesar for lunch, and a steak or burger for dinner filled the bill nicely.

As I headed to the fundraiser, my stomach churned with hunger and the uncertainty of seeing Melissa in person again. Being a private eye, I put on my professional face and decided that I'd just do my suave, debonair, man-about-town routine so that I wouldn't be out of place or worse, break into a sweat when she and I crossed paths.

I pulled the Monster into the garage adjacent to the hotel and walked across the street. I never valeted the Monster. I didn't appreciate the ripples of laughter and guffaws from the driver taking her away, anymore than the gaggle of tow trucks that followed the Monster wherever I went, like vultures waiting for an old man to die in the desert.

Entering the hotel, I quickly scanned the lobby and followed the other penguins and ladies in waiting down to the Spanish Ballroom.

It was a swanky spread to say the least. The foyer had been turned into a small New England fishing village, complete with faux grass, turn-of-the-century gas streetlights, shops and rowboats brimming with oysters on the half shell and gulf prawns.

I may not be a fancy food kind of guy, but my stint in the Keys taught me to love seafood. I had found nirvana.

I grabbed a plate and loaded it with prawns and oysters. As I scarfed down dinner I exchanged pleasantries and acknowledging glances with the rich and famous of Seattle.

Then I spotted Melissa across the room, at least I thought it was her. If it weren't for her gorgeous gold main of hair, I may not have recognized her. She was stunning from top to bottom. Absolutely ravishing, dressed in a skin tight evening dress that dropped down to her belly button before surrendering completely and falling to the floor. Oh, to be the material in that dress.

She caught me staring. I smiled back and made my way over to her.

"Melissa, you look absolutely amazing," I said, my eyes roaming up and down her slender frame and fetching assets.

"Eyes. Two. Up here," she said, bringing a swift end to my trance. "Like what you see, eh? Amazing what you can do when you're loaded. Seems they can fix just about everything with enough money. Except your personality, perhaps."

"I must say, Melissa, you are quite the eye candy these days. I should have never let you go."

"Your loss, baby," she replied, before taking a long sip from her champagne glass. "Never judge a book by its cover when someone is still editing it. So, what brings you to an event that I know kills you to be at?"

"Direct as ever, I see. O.K. then. I'm working on a case and I need your help," I replied, a bead or two of sweat working its way down my forehead. "You used to work with the information services folks at Associated Grocers back when you were still at Microsoft, didn't you?"

"Yeah, but that was a lifetime ago. How could that even remotely connect me to anything you could possibly be working on?"

"I'd rather not go into much detail here as it's a private matter. Can we meet at your house tomorrow, say around 1-ish? It won't take long, promise."

"That'd be fine," she said. "But I have a massage penciled for 2 so don't be late. And it had better be good, Brew or I'll make sure that your donation tonight gets tripled by the time it clears the bank."

"Donation?"

"If you want to keep your one o'clock with me, it'll be sizeable."

I walked away in a bit of a panic. As I said, even my

power bill was delinquent. How would I get some dough for the donation?

I thought for a moment, then dashed off a check for the fundraiser, a cool $500, post-dated two days. That would give me enough time to hock the Rolex Melissa had given me as a gift for services, um, rendered, and cover the check and then some. Ah, the price of transient lust wearing love as a disguise.

Chapter 7

Traffic was backed up as usual on 520. The floating bridge was built in the early 1960s when no one ever dreamed that the population would explode beyond the borders of sanity as prosperity continued to strike the Puget Sound.

Not so many years ago you could navigate the entire corridor at just about any time of day without even tapping the brakes. Now, the traffic copters hovered over the interchanges on the weekends. A bad sign.

Fortunately, I was a native and had prepared for the possibility that traffic would suck, so I left at 11, leaving plenty of time to make the once quick trip to Medina.

At a quarter to one, I made the turn onto the private drive and headed toward the beachside gates. This wasn't exactly new territory for me but I still marveled at the view Melissa had of the lake and the Seattle skyline beyond every time I came here. The view from my own housienda was less inspirational – the back wall of the Puget Sound Co-op.

Her estate used to belong to Governor Evans after he left office. It was a Greek Revival, with stunning columns lining the entryway. I always thought it looked more like a mausoleum than a mansion. The place gave me the creeps whenever I stayed there.

Yes, stayed there. Melissa may have had something

left to be desired in the looks department when we dated, but in a dark room, she was quite enjoyable. And who was I to turn down the slightly kinky advances of one of the wealthiest women in the U.S.?

I parked the Monster on the circular drive behind her classic 350SL. The Monster looked a little out of place, but so was its driver.

I knocked on the door and the maid let me in. She led me to the study and closed the French doors behind me. I made myself at home and did what I usually do when I'm in an office alone. I sat down and started to read everything on her desk.

This is an art I had picked up when I moved into the detective side of Seattle police work. Being dyslexic, I had learned that I could read upside down almost as fast as I could read right side up. So I could sit during a meeting with anyone and glance at their desk while they were on the phone or otherwise distracted.

"Stop reading, McCabe," I heard from behind me. "I know your little trick."

Caught in the act. And worse yet, I had let my guard down. As I was lost in the moment of prying into her life, she had stealthily entered through a side entry and came in behind me.

"So are we here to learn what I'm up to these days or are we here to discuss what you need from me? As I said last night, I don't have a lot of time today for your usual, and might I add, somewhat predictable behavior."

I still couldn't stop staring at her, knowing that her looks now matched her talents. Geez, why had I been so shallow back then, or even last week? I shouldn't have broken her heart.

"You didn't break my heart, McCabe."

Damn! I gotta stop thinking out loud.

I pulled out the photo and handed it to her.

"Yeah, I know a couple of them," she said, even before I asked. "That's Shawn there in the back and Frank in the front, hamming it up as he always does."

"Do you know the guy in the suit by any chance?"

"No, but he looks a little out of place, doesn't he? Hey, isn't that, now what was her name – Laura, Lori, no, Lola – that's it – in the front? We used to shoot the breeze now and then while the guys were installing the hardware."

"She's dead, ya know."

Melissa staggered a little before finding the comfort of her leather chair. "Geez, Brewster. I didn't know. Was that the woman they found at Green Lake? I don't think I've ever known a dead person before. What do these people in the photo have to do with Lola's demise?"

"I'm not sure but this is my only lead so far," I said. "I'm trying to track down the guy in the suit. As you said, he's totally out of place."

She paused for a moment, staring deep at each of the faces in the photo.

"Well, I don't know who porky is but perhaps Frank will. After he was canned he decided to go into broadcasting. KCPQ hit him up to be a technology pundit and analyst on TV. He does a weekly bit on

what's hot and what's not in personal computing now.
Sorry I can't be more help."

"You've been a big help Melissa. Every little piece of
information helps. I'm going to follow up with Frank
and see where all this leads."

I kissed her lightly on the cheek and left. I never quite
know how to handle casual intimacy with women,
particularly those whom I've, well, um, you know. I
mean, do you hug them? Kiss them? And if so, how
intense? How long? Like you would your aunt at
Christmas time? Like your sister? Or perhaps, like your
best female friend that you never were able to get into
the sack?

So confusing. I thought the cheek was a nice touch.
Friendly, but not too friendly. I suppose I could have
just groped her for old time's sake. You really couldn't
blame me. She really had it all now and she knew it.
Damn!

I hopped back into the Monster, cursing my luck and
my shallow nature and drove away. As I did, I
wondered if she had any money left, given the
remodeling job. The new boobs alone must've cost her
a mint. But I had to admit they were worth every dime.

I drove over to the TV station where Frank worked
now. I had hoped to catch him there, preparing for the
5 o' clock broadcast.

It was located in the Denny Regrade, not far from the
Dog House. As luck would have it, Frank was in. The
receptionist gave me directions to his office, just down
the corridor, two quick rights, a zig then a zag, then a

left and a right just past the women's restroom.

After three wrong turns, including the women's restroom, I found his office.

He was hunched over his computer, keying in his commentary. He was a lanky fellow, with black hair, wire glasses and, judging by the awards, plaques and photos consuming every empty space in his small office, had an ego the size of Detroit.

"Can I help you?" he asked, looking up from his screen with more than a slight amount of disdain.

"You used to work with Lola Chase at Associated Grocers didn't you?"

"Why yes. I heard she's dead. Who are you, the police?"

"A private Investigator," I replied. "Lola was an acquaintance and I'm following up on a few leads."

"Sit down, won't you?"

I moved a stack of *PC Worlds* and *InfoWeeks* from the only chair in the room and took my place across from Frank.

I handed him the photo, hoping he'd remember the occasion. He looked at it for a moment or two, then handed it back.

"Let's be frank, uh, Frank," I said. "Do you remember this day?"

"Sure I do. Like it was yesterday. We were at the park for our annual IT department picnic. You know, the usual assortment of meaningless team building exercises, rah-rah speeches and overcooked, dry hamburgers.

"Lucky for us Shawn had smuggled in some vodka and we were all doped up on Purple Hooters. Funny how booze can bond really different people together – just look at those in the photo."

"What do you mean, Frank?"

"Well, here's Shawn. Fresh out of college, ambitious and a bit of a butt kisser. He reported to me and desperately wanted my job. Then there's the buxom blond here in the bikini, Becky. Not an ounce of brains but the CEO's niece. So she gets a cushy job in information technology without any expectations. And of course, no one wanted to cross her because of her uncle."

"Go on," I said.

"Here's Jason. He was a bit of an alcoholic and womanizer. He fretted more about his receding hairline than his lack of knowledge of computing networks. Last I heard he was going through his third round of rehab and umpteenth hair weave."

"What do you know about the guy in the suit?" I asked, hoping he'd know.

"Oh, him. Geez, he was a strange duck. Worked in the mailroom down the hallway on the first floor. He was a reclusive kind of guy. Kept to himself mostly. If I remember, Lola was just about the only person who'd talk to him at the company. Everyone else thought he was a bit of a whack."

"What was he doing at the picnic?"

"Oh, Lola was always picking up strays," he continued. "This was just another one of her projects.

The picnic continued into the after work hours and she invited Darryl – yeah, that was his name – to come over after he made the last mail run. Geez, almost forgot about him."

"What's up with the suit he's wearing?" I asked. "Everyone else is in shorts. He's a real standout, but not for very good reasons."

Frank went back to work on his piece for the news, but continued his commentary on the photo as he tapped on the keyboard.

"If I recall, he was always dressed that way at work. We were business casual there, but old Darryl always wore a suit. Not a nice suit mind you; it was usually kind of rumpled. I think it made him feel like he was one of our equals, even though he was just Darryl, the Mailroom Guy. It looks like he must have stopped by the KFC drive-thru on the way to the picnic. I guess he didn't know that the boss had already picked up the tab for all the food."

"So what kind of guy was he? Do you think he'd have a reason to hurt Lola?"

"I don't think he'd hurt a living soul," Frank said. "I think he had a crush on Lola. But who didn't? She was quite the woman. Easy going. Pleasing to look at. Seemed to like just about everyone. But would Darryl harm her? Nah. Can't picture it…"

"How long did he work at Associated Grocers?"

"He was there until a year ago, I think. He originally made the move to Vancouver when the company went through its merger. Then they reorganized the shipping department and he was let go. Beyond that, I really don't know much about him. We weren't exactly friends."

I thanked Frank for his time and decided it was time to find out what Darryl's story was.

I headed back to my office, knowing that a trip to Vancouver was in my near future, very near future, in fact.

That's Vancouver, Washington, not Canada. Vancouver is about 15 minutes from Portland, on the north side of the Columbia River. A lot of my family was originally from there so I was pretty familiar with the lay of the land. But this time, I wouldn't be there for pleasure. Of course, with my family it was never a pleasure either.

I called down to the company's headquarters and made an appointment to speak to their HR Director. When asked what the reason for my appointment was, I gilded the lily a bit by saying that I was performing a background check for a food retailer. I just needed to go over a few facts about the applicant.

Next, I called Finchley and asked him to join me for dinner. He had been checking out Bubba's story and keeping Grist occupied with some diversions.

Actually I was trying to keep Finchley as far away from me as possible. I liked him, we were best friends, but lately I liked him better in small doses. Tonight would be one of those doses.

We met at the Admiral Benbow Inn, a quirky restaurant next to the TNT. I'd been eating there for years and it was a good place to eat gritty steak and chew the fat with a friend.

We took refuge in the Benbow's Hispaniola bar. If this all sounds a bit Treasure Island, it's no coincidence. The bar is loosely based on the ship in the book, complete with the reflections of waves on the back windows of what would be the captain's quarters on a real sailing vessel.

Finchley arrived about 10 minutes after I did.

"Hey boss. How's things on your side of the fence?"

"Fine, Finch. I have a lead on the guy in the suit and am heading down to Vancouver in the morning."

"I love the money there," he said, taking a seat across from me. "It's so colorful compared to ours. I just wish it was easier getting through the border."

"I mean the one in Washington, Finchley, not Canada. I'm following a lead tomorrow. One of the guys in the photo identified porky – his name is Darryl – and he worked in the mailroom at what used to be Associated Grocers before United Grocers sucked the corporate life out of them in a merger. He and Lola were acquaintances.

Finchley kicked back in his chair and gave me a knowing wink.

"Gotcha McCabe. A lead, uh-huh. I really thought you were into the ladies but if it's a guy who floats your romantic boat, no biggy to me, as long as it's not me, that is."

"Can you tell me what you're taking, Finch? It's got to be pretty powerful stuff because I think it's killed all but two brain cells in that head of yours. They really were friends you dumb ass, not lovers. Is your mind always in the gutter?"

Thankfully, my third round arrived just in time to save him from finding my fist shoved down into his mouth instead of the deluxe burger the barmaid had set down in front of him.

"So, Finchley, old boy," I said. "What have you found out?"

He began to mumble something about Bubba. Then he realized his mouth was full. Gulping, he repeated his report.

"Bubba was out with his friends, that's for sure. I met with a couple of two-bit businesses in the Central District who were reluctant to speak with me. They kept looking around as we talked. Like someone was watching their every move.

"But they did point to his photo as being one of the 'bill collectors' that night. Said he was with two or three other guys."

I was both relieved and disappointed that he wasn't a suspect any longer. Relieved I wouldn't have to try to bring the Incredible Bulk to justice and disappointed that perhaps he really did love Lola after all.

"So that takes him out," I said dejectedly, taking an extra long sip of bourbon. "What has Grist been up to?"

"He has a couple detectives following me around from time to time. He seems to be occupied with police biz down at the precinct."

"Do you think he knows what we know?"

"And that is…"

"Everything I told you this evening, Finchley. For cryin' out loud, were you a breech birth or somethin' because you're always behind on things."

"Sorry chief. I think he knows as much as the morgue report told him."

Geez, I almost forgot the autopsy.

"Can you use your contacts downtown to get a copy of the report while I'm in Vancouver?" I said. "We need to get an official cause of death."

"You bet, boss," he replied, with a mock salute. "I'm on it."

Chapter 8

The drive to Vancouver is a boring one at best. Outside of the dual Hicksvilles of Centralia and Chehalis, there's not much between Seattle and Vancouver to see.

The drive took just over two and a half hours. Thankfully, they had kicked the speed limit up to 65 a few years back so the drive was much less painful and plodding than it was at double nickels.

I pulled into the company's lot about 10 a.m. and collected my visitor's badge at the front desk. Jim met me a few minutes later. He was the HR Director and he led me up to the next floor and down a long corridor to his office.

"Thanks for taking the time to meet with me on such short notice," I said, as he ushered me into his corner office.

"No problemo!" he said, disgustingly happy. "Always ready to be of help."

Jim looked to be in his early 50s. I could tell Jim was a bit of a stiff shirt. Not just because he was wearing one but because everything about him was obsessively tidy, right down to his desk. I swear he had used a t-square and level to align everything on it. It was unsettlingly precise.

The numerous awards on the wall were no different. I was glad that I hadn't been there to interview for a job because I would have quickly cracked under the pressure of trying to fit into the very small box he seemed to judge everyone by.

"Mr. Davis, let me cut to the chase," I began. "I represent a large retailer that is ready to move aggressively into the Seattle market. They're going to be really big, really fast. And let's just say that they could become a very large customer of your company, if the, um, level of mutual trust is there."

Jim leaned back in his chair, instantly aware that he could score a business coup for the company by being forthcoming with the information I sought.

"I see no problem with that, Mr. McCabe, is it?" he said, leaning back into his desk, hands clasped as if he were praying.

"So we understand one another," I said, nodding. "Good, then let's get down to it."

I started to lay it on real thick, telling the tale of the non-existent European retailer that had a new store concept that was going to take the market by storm. Big plans, aggressive marketing, big support from supplier-partners, six figure salaries for the management team with bonuses – the works.

It was just the bait I needed. He hung on every word. I could see dollar signs dancing in his eyes. HR guys love an insider's tip on a possible investment. It was a nice change of pace from hiring mindless drones to fill endless cubicles in faceless business parks.

He leaned in even more, nodding in excitement. "Oh, yes, I've heard rumors about them. So, you're telling me that it's really true – coming to market that is."

"Before the holidays, of course," I smiled.

He shot backwards in his chair. Fish on! I had hit the jackpot. The holiday selling season. All I had to do now was secure the hook and reel him in.

"So what can I possibly do to be of assistance, Mr. McCabe?" he said, almost salivating. "Would you like a soda or something else perhaps?"

I took the moment to seize control of the conversation.

"No, Mr. Davis. What I need most is information. As you know, one can't be too careful in this business."

I shifted my glance back and forth in his office, like I was looking out for the prying eyes of spies.

"Oh, yes, you don't have to tell me," he replied. "There are a lot of *bad eggs* out there."

Retail grocery humor, how quaint.

"Well, now that we are in agreement, we are looking at hiring a new person to head our shipping operation. I understand that he worked in your mailroom up until a year ago and I want to get some background info on him. His name is…

I glanced down at my notebook. Spiral notebooks are such a handy thing. They lend an instant air of authority to any situation. When I was in college at the University of Washington, I was able to get onto the football field with nothing more than a notebook in my hand, a harried look on my face and purposeful, athletic-shoed feet to carry me by security. They never questioned me – they figured I had to either be with the visiting team, the home team or the band. Try it some time. Carry a notebook or clipboard anywhere and you'll find you gain instant respect. As long as you look like you know what you're doing, why you're there and where you're going, you can go just about anywhere.

As for me, it led me to Jim. And he was about to spill his guts.

I looked up from the notebook, with a detached, searching look. "Oh yes, Darryl, that was his name… Darryl…"

"Diamond," Jim volunteered. "Darryl Diamond! He worked in our mailroom before and after our move to Vancouver. Strange guy but damned good at his job. He was a bit of a health risk for the company…"

"Health risk?" I said, surprised.

"Well, between you and I, yes. He was quite a big boy. He could fill up the mail van all by himself, if you know what I mean."

"So you say he left the company. When did he leave and why?"

"I'm not really supposed to share that information, you know, Mr. McCabe. It's confidential. We don't want to open ourselves to any lawsuits because of it, especially with my crack about his girth versus worth."

Without a word, I rose to my feet. The chair chattered across the floor as I stood, making a shrill noise that made you want to claw your eyes out.

"Well thank you for your time, Mr. Davis. I think our

business is concluded then. My client will be disappointed that you weren't able to be of more help."

I turned to walk away and felt Jim grab my arm.

"Let's not be so hasty, there, Mr. McCabe. Please have a seat."

The prospect of making a killing in the market had tipped the scales of sound judgment in my favor. I went in for the kill.

"Thanks Jim," I said, making myself comfortable. "I'm glad you can be of assistance. I think my client will consider you in a very favorable light in the coming months." I leaned into his desk. "And you just never know, they may be in the market for a new VP of Human Resources.

"So, let's talk about our mutual friend, Darryl, shall we?" I continued. "What can you tell me Jim that will be of use to the company I represent?"

Jim excused himself for a few moments and left the room.

I glanced once more around his pristine office. I just couldn't stand it any longer. I got out of my chair and tilted a couple of the awards hanging on the wall behind his desk.

I heard the doorknob begin to turn and sat back down, leaning back in my chair. Jim re-entered with a folder in his hand.

He immediately noticed that the frames were askew and I could tell it was really bothering him. After all, he had left them in perfect order only a moment ago.

"I have to level with you," he said, as he glanced at

Darryl's files. "Darryl was a model employee," he said. "He started in the mailroom as a Grade 9 and moved steadily through the ranks, from driver to Senior Mailroom Clerk III by the time he left our employment last July."

"Where did he go after leaving here?"

"We don't have those kinds of records, Mr. McCabe," Jim replied a queer grin telling me he was lying.

I smiled back at him, looking him directly in the eye. "Of course there are ways, Mr. Davis. You know it and I know it. There are unemployment claims with addresses on them, requests for references, employment checks, credit checks, etc."

I got up to leave again as his conscience fought another round with his insatiable greed.

"Why of course, Mr. McCabe, of course! How silly of me. Those are in the other file on Darryl. Just one moment."

He opened his door and called to his secretary. Oh, I can hear what you're saying… how unprofessional of me to call her a secretary. At least I didn't call her a dame.

"Miss Morton," he called. "Can you bring me the other file on Darryl Diamond?"

"What other file?" came the reply. "You have the only file that we have on him."

I could hear Jim sigh in embarrassment as he closed the door. He was looking for anything to cover his tracks. He slowly made his way back to his chair, then got a look on his face like he had discovered the cure for smallpox.

"Oh, of course!" he said, with a forced look of astonished triumph on his face. "I forgot that we had combined all the records into single files after the move here. How silly of me."

"Yes, how silly," I offered, mocking his tone.

He reopened the file, shuffled through a few more papers and then looked up at me. A bead of sweat trickled down his brow.

"There was a request for confirmation of employment from the Belltown unemployment office in Seattle last August," he slowly spat out. "His request was approved by the state since his leaving was due to relocation of the company and he continues to receive benefits today."

"And his current address is?"

"Wait," he replied, haltingly. "Wouldn't you already know that Mr. McCabe? I'd assume it would have been on his application to your client's company."

The jig was up. I sprang from the chair and grabbed Jim by his starched collar. I leaned in within inches of his face.

"Look you slimy little bastard," I said. "I'm tired of your horseshit games. You and I both know what's going on here. And if you cooperate, you just may live through this day. I don't have a lot of patience right now. I had to drive all the way down here to kiss your sorry ass. Do you know what that means, asshole? Centralia and Chehalis. I'm right on the edge, shithead. I had to go through those hellholes and burn up a tank and a half of gas I won't get reimbursed for, just to have your puny, self-important little executive ass give me the runaround!"

I pushed him as I released his collar and he fell back into his chair. As he started to reach for the intercom he noticed that I had pulled my Redhawk from its holster. I jammed it into the base of Jim's nose.

"And the Final Jeopardy answer is... Jim?"

"What is 685 Somerset Place SE, Bellevue, Washington?"

"Phone number?"

"None listed."

I shoved the barrel deeper into his snot box.

"No, really! I'm telling the truth. See for yourself!"

I snatched the folder from his hand, then returned the gun to my holster. "There's only two things I believe in, Jimbo. I believe in justice being served and payments that clear."

"McCabe, you'll pay for this one day," he said, as he collapsed in his chair.

"Pay for what? The clean bill for that puddle of piss in your chair? Have a great day, Jim. I'll see myself out!"

I left Jim to his laundry problem and made my way back to the Monster. I jostled and jiggled the muddy ignition and slammed the car into gear. I peeled out of the lot, hoping that the security cameras wouldn't connect me with Jim's little wetting until I was well on my way to Bellevue. I had a feeling that he wouldn't want to pursue the matter, since he'd have to explain the sudden change of wardrobe back at the office and the aromatic scent of spent adrenaline and pee in his office.

I headed back onto I-5 and set the cruise control to a cool 69. I hedged my bets that the speedometer was accurate and used the time needed to get to Bellevue to recount the clues that had led me to cause a middle-aged man to wet his pants in broad daylight.

I yearned for a car phone, but they were prohibitively expensive, as all new gadgets are. Only the likes of Bill Gates could afford such things. Bastard! I would have to make due with the payphone 50 miles away at the next rest stop as I hated getting off the freeway for any reason outside of an empty gas tank. But I did need to check in with Finchley to see what the coroner's report had turned up. I hoped I had a quarter in my pocket.

As I went north, my mind went south. I started to think back to my younger, wilder days when I lived in Bellevue. I'm still not sure why I lived there. I'm not even sure how I slipped through its well-guarded borders.

I knew at a very early age that I wasn't Bellevue material. I had been rejected, not only personally, but on a geo-political-economic-societal level. You see, I grew up in Kennydale, a suburb of blue collar Renton sharing a border with blue nose Bellevue. It was like a nightmarish game of Red Rover, Red Rover, where Brewster McCabe would never be worthy of being sent over to the other side.

Not that growing up in Renton was so bad. O.K., so I'm lying. We're talking about Renton. We couldn't exactly call it South Bellevue to make it appear any nicer. It was a working class town with working class stiffs who toiled in their dead end jobs at Boeing, putting the same rivet in the same hole every day of their working lives, just so they could get a cake and a gold watch as they were shuffled out the door at 65. Left to live a retired life in a company town... rotting at the Senior Center, just a stone's throw away from the factory that churned out 727s and 737s seven days a week, 24 hours a day.

It always frightened me that roughly half of the world's airliners were assembled by people who lived and worked in Renton. Small wonder why these things mysteriously fall apart on takeoff, on landing or in midair – the people in Renton put them together.

I know what you're saying... you're being a bit harsh on your hometown. Don't get me wrong. It was a great place to be a kid. Back then you could tote a real machine gun around the neighborhood and no one thought twice about it. And you could go off for a day with your friends without fearing that some whacko would kill you in the woods. It was a very small town, filled with small crime. Unfortunately, it was also filled with small minds, most of them at Boeing.

When I was in high school in Renton, the drama department planned to put on a production of Tom Jones. No need to search through the ever dimming recesses of your mind to remember this production. Suffice it to say that at the time it had recently been done on Broadway "el nudo" and Boeing officials went nuts when they thought their sexually active sons and daughters were going to appear in a high school play in the buff.

So, they pulled the plug on the play. They didn't even

ask if it was going to be in the nude. Knowing most of the people in the cast at the time, nudity wouldn't have been a big attraction anyway. Not the most shapely Thespians at Hazen High in those years.

But once again, I digress.

After Renton annexed Kennydale, it and Bellevue suddenly shared a common border. But adjoining plots of taxable real estate was all they had in common. Bellevue was for the up and coming. Renton was for the down and out. People in Renton built the planes that only people from Bellevue could afford to fly in. They jetsetted about the world while the workers blew their weekly pay in less exotic places with names like the Melrose, Bunkhouse and Barei's. A quarter went a long way – a schooner could be had for two bits – a whole pitcher for $3. In a single afternoon, the working class could empty most of the kegs in town with Boeing paychecks. Most of the bars would even countersign the checks and hand any change left over at the end of the night to their highly inebriated customers as they stumbled toward the door at closing time.

When you were born in Renton, you were branded for life. No need to get a tattoo. Everyone knew your origins, just like those poor unfortunate souls born in places like Queens or Watts. It was the stench of a birthright that no amount of personal hygiene products could mask.

I don't think it would come as a surprise to the very few who knew me that I fled the town as soon as I could as an adult. The decision came, fittingly, on New Years Eve, 1973. I was at the Bunkhouse with a now ex-girlfriend, celebrating with friends. I had blown $12 on four pitchers of beer to help dull the pain of spending the last moments of the year in a dingy bar surrounded by equally dingy working class stiffs.

As the country band blared out an off-key rendition of Auld Lang Syne, I looked around the room. Everything was moving in slow motion, perhaps because of the beer, perhaps because it's one of those defining moments in your life when you see your future as clear as a bell. I saw my entire life laid out before me. And it wasn't pretty. It was a dull existence, one where I would spend my remaining days in the same town, with the same friends, greeting old schoolmates I never liked in the first place at the neighborhood grocery store, going to little league games and telling these same people that their kid was terrific at bat, even though they swung at air all day, driving to and from work in an old Pinto wagon...

AHHHHHH!

I broke out in a cold sweat. I suddenly stood up and left the bar, my friends, my girlfriend and the town. I vowed never to return until I made something of my life. I never really thought it would take this long.

Funny how much your mind can wander in just 50 miles. I pulled off at the Toutle River rest stop, pulled a quarter from my pocket and dialed Finchley. As usual, he didn't answer, meaning I'd have to leave yet another message on his answering machine and hope that he remembered how to access it remotely. Talk about someone who could use a mobile phone.

Finally, civilization. Well, sort of. I exited off I-5 and drove up 405 through the S-curves, passing through my old hometown. I could see that same Renton bar I had stepped out of only a few years earlier. It was now boarded up. For all I knew owner Virgil was long gone by now. Even in life, it could be hard to tell if Virgil was alive or dead on any particular night. He drank right along with the patrons, chain smoked at least three packs of Marlboros a day and swore like the sailor he was. And in the years I frequented the place to drink the cheap beer, listen to country *and* western music and shoot some pool on a sagging table where all the balls rolled to the center, I never once saw ol' Virg ever step out from behind the bar. If he's dead, they probably just boarded the place up and left him there, still standing behind the bar as stiffly in death as in life.

Traffic on 405 was amazingly light today. I easily transited to the Coal Creek exit and followed the directions on my gas station map to the address Jim had been so kind to give me. Finally, I was going to meet up with the ever-elusive Darryl.

The address really wasn't that hard to figure out. Somerset Place was in Somerset, a hillside development built in the 1960s that was supposed to be a model for all planned communities. Everything in the neighborhood was pristine. The lawns, freshly manicured. Matching mailboxes set street side, just so. The homes were all slightly different in style, but built from the same basic plan sets. It was very Stepford Wives. The only thing the planners hadn't planned was the streets. They wove in and out of the community, some looping around on themselves, others coming to a dead end. Well, that's what we called them when I was a kid. In Bellevue, they simply put a slab of circular pavement at the end and called it a "Court." I guess people here wouldn't buy an overpriced home on a dead end. But call it a court and viola!, instant sale above the asking price.

After turning the Monster around in numerous courts, tracking back down the same roads I came in on and cursing the map, then crossing back and forth through nonsensical, meandering streets, I finally found Somerset Place. I pulled to a stop on the corner. From here I could see the house Darryl listed as his last address and do a little reconnaissance work before moving in.

Nothing happened for the next two hours. Well, things might have happened but I wouldn't have known it - I had dozed off at the wheel. I awoke as a car passed me. It turned into the driveway of the house. I pretended not to stir as I peered out from under my fedora. The driver got out of the car - the car springing back to level in relief - and headed into the house. The time had come to meet my primary suspect.

I cranked up the Monster and eased down the road, blocking the car in the driveway to prevent any possible escape. Things were about to get a little heated and I didn't need a high-speed chase to deal with through the spaghetti roads of Somerset. In the heat of a pursuit I would never find my way out of here, even under the best of terms.

I walked up to the door and knocked. The panes in the windows shook gently, reflecting the obvious stress the floors of the house were under as the person came to the door.

I was speechless. There standing before me wasn't the person I expected. Just as grandiose in scale, mind you, but he was a she.

"Can I help you?" she asked.

"I... I..." I stuttered as I tried to regain my composure. "I'm Brewster McCabe. I am investigating a murder and wanted to ask Darryl Diamond a few questions. Is he here?"

"Is he in trouble or something?"

"No, no. The person who was murdered was a mutual friend of ours and I just thought he could help me sort a few things out."

"Well, he's not here," she replied. "I'm his sister, Darla. Is there something I could do for you?"

Wishing to get any tidbit I could for my trouble coming here, I accepted her offer to come in.

She excused herself for a moment, saying she needed to get ready for work. As she turned, I couldn't help but check her out as she went down the narrow hall of the house. Well, the hall wasn't that narrow. She just filled most of it. She was wearing a pair of cutoff denim shorts that didn't cover her cheeks and a blue tank top. Not my usual taste – not that I really had any – but surprisingly, I found myself oddly aroused.

She returned a few moments later. She had traded the t-shirt for a V-neck red sweater and the shorts for a black leather mini skirt and sky-high boots. Fetching. Even though she was BBW, I thought she could also be BB-Doable.

"Sorry, but I just came home to change," she said apologetically. "I need to get to work down at the Lazy Susan."

"The strip club?" I asked.

"Yeah, that's the one. There's a convention in town and I'm doing a special appearance there tonight."

"A convention, huh? Overeater's Anonymous?"

"So you heard they were here, huh? Anyway, they like a certain style of entertainment. It's not glorious work, but it pays the bills around here. Especially since Darryl hasn't found a job yet and isn't much help, when he's around, that is."

My mind wandered between the need to be professional and the need to explore Darla's assets. The spinner stopped back on Darryl.

"Do you know where he is now, Darla?"

"Nah, I never know from one minute to the next where he is. He only stays here occasionally these days. Mostly when he's not getting any up in Canada, if you know what I mean."

"Canada? Does he live there?"

"Hell if I know, McCabe. I'm hardly my brother's keeper these days. He's a bit of a deadbeat in my book. I'm sure he's up there shagging his life away. He's quite the man's man," letting go a laugh.

"When was he last here?"

"Last night, actually. He came in around 1 a.m., his mistress in hand."

"A girlfriend?"

"No, silly," she replied, as she turned to look at me. "A bucket of the Colonel's finest. He just loves that fried chicken."

She came towards me. She adjusted her breasts a bit as she moved. Then she licked her lips ever so gently.

"Are you hungry, Brewster?"

"Hungry for what?" I replied, somewhat afraid of the answer.

"You know. You want some? I have a few minutes. Wouldn't you just love to wrap your mouth around a breast or maybe a thigh?"

"Well, now that you mention it, I would like some of that. I haven't had any for some time."

"I'll be back in a jiff," she said, disappearing once more.

I loosened my tie and removed my jacket. I sank down into the velvet couch and wondered what she'd be like in the sack. Somewhere in the back of my mind I had always wondered what it would be like with a big boned babe, but I had never had the pleasure of checking that off my list.

I removed my shoes, loosened the garters and took off my socks. As I was unbuttoning my trousers, Darla returned to the room.

She dropped the plate of chicken on the floor and screamed.

"What the hell are you doing, you sicko? Get the hell out of my house before I call the cops!"

I stumbled to my feet, trying to grab my clothes as I stood.

"When you mentioned breasts and thighs, I assumed you wanted a little of the ol' Brewster here."

"I was talking about the Colonel, you idiot. Darryl left some of his chicken in the fridge."

"Please forgive me," I said. "It was a complete misunderstanding."

Darla started to laugh as she bent down to pick up the chicken, now mixed into the shag carpet with some coleslaw and mashed potatoes.

"Why is it that every guy in the world gets a hard on for us larger than life women?" she said. She looked at me. "Do you think we compensate in other ways, such as being wild in the sack?"

I was blushing from head to toe. "Uh, perhaps!"

"Well, let me tell you something Mr. McCabe. It's all true!" letting go another laugh. "I'm not easy, but I can be had and boy, is it worth it!

"If it wasn't for this convention being in town and having to work, I'd probably let you revel in this bodacious body just so you could find out how strong your heart is."

"Well, I should go now," I said, wishing to make as hasty and as graceful exit as I could.

"What's the hurry sweets? You're kind of cute standing there half naked and as embarrassed as a teenager caught in the act of whacking off in the locker room. Now you've given me a good case of the hornies. Are you sure you want to miss out on a little of this?"

I admit, I was very tempted to check this off my bucket list. She was all go, go, go but I had to say no.

"Sorry, I really need to get back to work."

I didn't get far. As I turned to say goodbye, she fell on me, pinning me to the floor. Before I knew it, my drawers were off again and she had hopped on for a little ride.

I would like to say that I put up a good fight, but I

didn't. It had been a while since my last horizontal mambo and I was all in. I closed my eyes and fantasized that Darla was Lola, when she was alive that is.

She finished before I could and without further ado, hopped off the Brewster train at the next stop. I hadn't had time to arrive at the station yet myself, but she couldn't have cared less. She had already gotten off.

"Perhaps we'll meet again," she replied, adjusting her skirt. "Want another piece before you go?"

I didn't know what she meant and I was not about to make the same mistake twice.

She took the lead. "You look like a leg man, McCabe. Here's a drumstick for the road."

She stuck the drumstick in my now gaping mouth and shut the door. As I walked back to the car, I could hear a roar of laughter coming from inside the house. Things just couldn't get any worse, I thought.

Chapter 9

They could.

After 30 more minutes of courts, cul-de-sacs and switchbacks, I found my way out of Somerset. I could have just waited for Darla to leave for work and follow her back. But the laughter cascading from the house bruised my pride. So I opted to go it alone.

I stopped at a payphone at a nearby gas station. I dialed Finchley's pager this time and waited for him to give me a ring back. I waited. And waited. Then waited some more. I paged him again.

Fifteen minutes went by before the phone finally rang. I picked up the receiver.

"Hey boss," came the reply. "You wanted something?"

"Why yes, Finchley," that's why I paged you. "Did you get the pages I sent?"

"Yeah, I did. Took me a while to figure out what what was causing the vibrating. Thought it was a seizure or something at first. Good thing it wasn't. My Aunt Sophie had one of those once and she started foaming at the mouth and then her eyes rolled up into the back of her..."

"Can we cut out the medical history of your family, Finchley? I'd rather have the coroner's final report, remember? Did you get the report?"

"You bet, McCabe. I've got it right here."

"Good!" I said. "Meet me back a the office and we'll go over it."

I hung up the phone and got back into the Monster. Just as I turned over the engine, a familiar car drove by. It was the one from the house. I decided to tail it for a while, just out of curiosity.

I kept a comfortable distance, even though she'd probably seen the Monster. It wasn't exactly stealthy.

We were obviously heading toward the Lazy Susan, so I didn't have to work too hard at keeping up *and* out of sight. They did a brisk lap dance business there with conventioneers, pilots and business travelers who filled the low rent hotels in the area.

The car pulled off the interstate and made a loop onto 99. The Lazy Susan was on the right, but Darla didn't stop there. Instead, she headed south down 99. I slipped in behind a taxi and continued to follow the car. I don't think I had been detected. Yet it was odd that Darla didn't turn into work, but continued on to a destination as of yet unknown.

She finally pulled off the highway and into the parking lot of the Bull Pen, a seedy karaoke bar that had seen better days along the interstate. It was classic 50s kitsch. The place looked like a castle, with a large plastic bull on the top of the tower near the highway. I heard that it was once known as the Spanish Castle in its glory days, when 99 was the only highway that could take you from the Canadian border to Portland, Oregon. When the new interstate was built, 99 had joined the ranks of other stretches of old highways that once thrived off our penchant for travel on a five dollar full tank of gas: Route 66, the El Camino, The Dixie Overland Highway, the list goes on.

I circled the block and eased into a parking spot in the back. I wasn't sure that I should go in or not. If the place was full I would have no trouble finding a spot to see what was going on. If it was a slow night, I'd stick out like a cross-dresser at an evangelical convention.

I decided it would be better to wait in the car. Thankfully, it was not a long wait. I watched her wave goodbye to someone in the bar and then pull away. Whoever she had met was still inside.

It was time to move. I let Darla go on her way, thinking she had just stopped off for a quick drink and some company before heading over to the Lazy Susan for a night of pole dancing. I hoped their pole was anchored deep in concrete. Otherwise, several patrons would be killed tonight. I could just picture the morning headlines:

Three Overeaters Anonymous members
crushed to death in Lazy Susan

Oh, the humanity!

I entered the Bull from the rear. I took up a place near the kitchen area and ordered a beer as I kept my back to the room. Using the reflections on the blank TV screens, I surveyed the room behind me. It was indeed a slow night. Karaoke was still a few hours away and only the regulars seemed to be in the place.

How could I tell? Regulars just have a certain look to

them, no matter what the bar. Well, yes, a drunk one. But to the trained eye, it's more than that. They look like they belong in the place they patronize. Over time, they begin to become part of the décor of an establishment, blending in with the sun-faded beer signs on the walls, the puke stained carpet and the cigarette burned bar.

Casual patrons always stand out. They clash with the decor. They don't know the system – how to get a drink or where the pissers are located. And there's no way they can act like a regular, no matter how hard they try.

There were only a few casuals in the room on this night. I picked them off one by one in the TV's reflection, then turned slowly to focus my attention on the chosen few.

In the corner was a hooker with her john. She was busy laughing at whatever he said while rubbing his leg with a pair of stilettos. With a dame, you always wonder if all that dough you spend on dinner and drinks will let you get lucky later. With a hooker, it's a sure thing, and they're not going to want to eat, well, at least not dinner. Why spend a wad when you can just shoot it instead for a lot less money?

There were a couple suits in the center of the room. They were obviously there to quaff a few drinks before heading out on the town looking for some excitement. In the Sea-Tac area, they might as well get a hooker, too. That is about the only excitement in this part of town. Tomorrow, they will catch a morning flight and head back to their wives in some nondescript third world town in the Midwest. In the meantime, they'll try to figure out how to finesse the most fun out of their limited expense accounts so they can justify their wanderlust to the main office.

Ah, yes, there's my target. Seated near the stage was a thin set man, a bit gaunt, and just a little tipsy. He must have been the one Darla was talking to. He looked a bit nervous as he sat there, thumbing through the karaoke songbook while looking periodically around the room, as if he had something to hide.

As he looked around, our eyes met. He smiled and acknowledged the awkward moment before putting his nose back into the book. I made a motion to the barmaid and made my way over to the table. He pretended not to notice my approach. I sat down across from him and said nothing. The barmaid was right behind me with a fresh supply of drinks.

"This is on the gentleman, sir," she said as she set his double scotch rocks on the table in front of him.

He didn't bother to look up. "Thanks," he said. "I needed this."

I asked him what he was thinking of singing tonight.

"Haven't given it much thought. You?"

"Not much of a singer," I replied. "I need a bar of soap and a washcloth before I'll warble a single note. Besides, this karaoke thing is a bit strange for me – another Japanese import that I can't understand."

He took another drink, a long one this time, emptying the glass. When he put it down, a smile briefly crossed his face. I motioned to the barmaid to bring another round to him.

He sat in silence for a few minutes more, nervously nursing the next drink, turning pages in the book and occasionally glancing around the room. He never once looked at me.

Finally, he decided I wasn't going to go away.

"So, to what do I owe the pleasure of your company – and the drinks?"

He hoisted his glass in a mock toast and finished off the second glass. This was turning out to be an expensive interrogation, particularly for a private eye who hasn't seen a decent check in a while.

"We have a mutual acquaintance I believe, mister…"

"Mister None of Your Damned Business," he replied curtly.

"Do you know a woman named Darla? Kind of a…"

"BBW?" he said, completing the thought.

"Why yes. Can you tell me how you came to know her?"

"Are you going to make it worth my while, friend?" he asked, signaling the barmaid for a third round on me.

"How about some stock in Johnnie Walker?"

He leaned forward in his chair. "Look, there's no reason to tell a total stranger about my relationships," he said. "Certainly not someone who looks and smells like a dick."

"Fair enough," I said.

I got up to leave.

He never saw it coming. I grabbed a full fist of his receding hairline and smashed his face into the table. The rings in the binder split open, cutting his nose. Splatters of blood covered the book and the table. I pulled his head back and slammed it back down again. The room grew quiet.

"Now, Mister Whatever Your Name Is. I'm a little tired of getting the runaround from every shithead I come into contact with today. I'm going to ask you one more time how you've come to know our mutual friend."

"I... I... I'm a regular at the Lazy Susan," he offered. "You could say I'm one of her best customers. She and I have had a thing on the side for some time now. Her husband doesn't know about it. Honest! Are you working for him?"

I let him go and sat back down. I handed him a couple cocktail napkins so he could wipe some of the blood from his face and motioned for a bar rag. I quickly seized on his mistake in my identity. "Yeah, that's it. I'm working for her husband."

The bar patrons returned to their own conversations. I lowered my voice as I continued.

"So, tell me about your little tryst with Darla. How long has it been going on?"

"Six months," he said. "A little more than six months. As I said, I met her at the Lazy Susan. She had been moved to the revolving stage they have and I loved to watch her do her act in the round. I have this thing for large women."

"Who doesn't?" I said, agreeing.

He continued. "One night, I was tipping pretty heavy. I had won some money on pull tabs and wanted to spread the wealth, if you get my drift. She was very appreciative. *Very* appreciative. So we ended up going back to my place and started fooling around. Nothing serious at first. But then it became a regular thing. I can't get her out of her mind."

"Did you ever meet her husband?"

"Yes, once. He came to pick her up at the Lazy Susan one night. She was a bit surprised to see him there. He usually didn't come down to the club because it was distasteful to him. He seemed friendly enough."

"And how did you come to see Darla this evening?"

"What do you mean? We haven't seen each other for a week."

Might as well go with what seems to be working. I pulled my pistol from its holster and pulled a Jim Davis. He raised his hands and backtracked.

"O.K., O.K., put that thing away. She was here a bit ago. We meet here regularly before she goes to work down the street. Just a quick drink and a few stolen moments. You aren't going to tell Darryl, are you?"

"Darryl? Why would I tell her brother?"

"What are you talking about, man? They're not siblings. Darla is Darryl's wife. Who told you otherwise?

"She did."

I left the asshole to clean off the mess I had created and headed back onto 99. The lights were with me for a change so it only took a few minutes to make my way back to the Lazy Susan.

I entered the dimly lit main lounge. The place was packed even though there were only nine people in it. I muscled my way past the plump rumps of the overachievers of Overeaters and took a seat stage-side.

A fetching young woman in not much more than a bra and g-string came over and took my drink order. After ordering up a couple Cokes and adding my own whiskey from my flask, I sat back and enjoyed the show, thankful that they had had the smarts to book skinny waitresses for this particular convention crowd. At least I'd get a drink here, even if it wasn't officially boozilicious.

That's the downside to Washington State. Strip clubs dot the landscape but there's no alcohol allowed. Soda only. Somewhere in our pioneer-Puritan minds we decided that nudity and booze weren't great mixers, so the liquor had to go if there was to be a show.

Not that I really enjoy the show at any strip club. To me, there's no point in going to a stripper bar. If you can't touch the merchandise and you can't take it home with you at the end of the night, why bother? I can usually see better breasts in a National Geographic. The dancing can be as uneven as those breasts, too. White girls, at least those taking their clothes off for a living, aren't necessarily great dancers. They are so busy gyrating and hugging the pole that they forget to listen to the music and count to four. Of course, that might be too much to ask some of these girls. Take off your clothes, dance, listen to the music *and* count. Four things to think about is simply too much for girls attracted to this line of business. At least the ones I've encountered over the years.

As the next show began, I thought about Lola. I had actually met her in a strip club across from the Drift On Inn a couple years ago. Of course, I didn't let Grist in on our history. I simply told him I knew her from

Dirk's. I was the one who was responsible for getting her the job there after convincing her that the life of a stripper wasn't for her. Waitressing didn't pay as well as getting naked in front of a bunch of salivating men, but at least it was relatively honest work.

Ah, I remember the day we first met. She was the headliner that night. I was tailing a client's husband. Seems he had a penchant for the young ladies at Sugar's. I must say, she was incredible. Her act consisted of two hula hoops, six pink ping pong balls and a large ear of corn. And when she...

Wait. A gentleman shouldn't tell such stories about the dead. Let's just say it was quite a show.

I don't know if she ever really missed showbiz. We never talked about it after she got the job at Dirk's. She seemed happy enough and the minimum wage and tips helped her pay the bills. I certainly was happier because I got to see her more often, albeit at a distance. Being the only waitress on her shift most of the time, she never had time to go much beyond the usual pleasantries and sporadic chitchat. It wasn't until that night at the TNT that I even knew about Bubba, the Caloric Caller and her pipe bombed Pinto.

Funny how the world works. She's gone and I'm back in a strip club, thinking of how we met while waiting for another woman, one who laid me out not more than a couple hours ago, to take her break.

One thing was for sure. In the dancing department it would take three Lolas to fill Darla's shoes and that wasn't a pretty thought at all.

It turns out I was wrong in this assumption. Darla took the stage and she was just as talented vertically as horizontally. Once the music ended, she took a bow, collected the wads of dollars and fivers on the floor, and came down to my table.

"Well, if it isn't the breast and thigh man," she said, a little out of breath from her performance. "Couldn't get enough of me, eh? What brings you here?"

"A friend of yours up at the Bull Pen."

"Dammit! Have you been following me? Geez, you're like some sicko Stalkerazzi. Is that how you get your jollies, McCabe?"

"Call it a hunch, but I wasn't too surprised that you didn't go directly to the Lazy Susan," I said, trying hard to be all business. "So, let's cut the shit. Why didn't you tell me that Darryl was your husband?"

"Steve told you that? That asshole." She stuffed some more of her take down her cleavage. "I can't believe he fell for that one in the first place. I just told him the husband story to add some mystery to our relationship and to keep him at arm's length. A gorgeous girl like me likes to keep her options open."

And legs, I thought to myself, but I choked the thought back down my throat and went in another direction. I didn't want to insult her, at least not at this particular moment.

"So, Darryl is…"

"My brother, like I said. Geez! Do you honestly think I would claim him as anything else? He's an overweight, do nothing son of a bitch."

I didn't know whether to believe her or not. The story seemed too convenient. Still, even if she was married to him it didn't really change things much. He was the one in the photo, not her. And the trail had led to him, not her. All she could do was shed some light on where he's been since he left for the Great White North and how he spent his time.

"What do you mean, a do nothing SOB? He worked didn't he?"

"He used to," she said. "He was in the mailroom at Associated Grocers. He even moved down to Vancouver for a while when they moved their headquarters there. But he didn't like Vancouver – thought it was a cultural wasteland."

I couldn't argue with that point.

"So he moved back here. He didn't have any place to stay so I said he could stay with me for a while. It took me forever to get rid of him."

"What do you mean?"

"He came here saying he wanted to find himself. So I offered him the spare bedroom I had. Over time he began to think the place was his instead of mine," she said. "He would constantly be munching down the groceries and never replace any of it. He'd drink the booze and never think to swing by the liquor store and pay me back. He's a bit of a leach. He only thinks of himself these days."

"You said, 'These days.' What does that mean?"

"Well, it wasn't always that way," she said, signaling g-string girl for a drink. "In the beginning, he was very helpful; he pulled his share of the load. I guess he was paying for everything with his severance checks because he never seemed to be in a hurry to get a job. He'd just sit around the house and watch cartoons. I'd come home and he'd have every video Disney ever made sprawled out in front of him. He'd just sit there, totally enraptured. When they were on, he wouldn't even notice anything else in the room. It was a bit creepy!"

"Did you ever call him on it?"

"Well, sure. He'd agree to pay rent and food and then nothing would ever come of it. After a while, I just gave up on him. Especially when he started getting really moody and even mean. I was afraid to confront him over even the littlest thing... afraid he'd just flip out on me."

"When did this happen?"

"It was about a year ago, I guess. "He changed virtually overnight. Like someone flipped a switch in him. The freak-out switch."

"Does he still stay with you?"

"Occasionally. I kicked him out of the spare bedroom and offered him the couch after he hightailed it to Canada with lover boy. The couch and the closet are about all he has here."

That was a pretty big couch she had in her house. I suppose it could hold him.

"Lover boy?" I asked.

"Look, I got to get back to work. The OA people are hungry for some of this," she said as she patted her rump.

Hope they brought a big appetite.

I thanked Darla and said I might need to see her again.

"You wouldn't be the first," she snapped.

She got that right.

Damn, I forgot that Finchley was waiting for me at the office. I glanced at my new Timex watch as I left. Thankfully, the Rolex was worth more than my donation to Melissa, so I had some extra scratch left over to buy a fine American watch manufactured in Japan. It was 9:30. My how time flies in a strip club.

I saw a phone booth over in the corner of the Lazy Susan parking lot. I reached into my pocket for a quarter and dialed the phone.

Suddenly, out of the corner of my eye, I caught the sight of the two headlights getting bigger by the second. They bounced wildly as the car flew over the speed bumps in the lot at top speed. The driver zeroed in on his target. I had but a moment to react. My keen private eye instincts kicked in. I timed my leap perfectly, crashing directly onto the hood of the vehicle, cracking the windshield with my forehead. As the car continued to dodge and weave through the lot with me as its hood ornament, I managed to slide off the passenger side, falling to the pavement as the car turned sharply to the left. I rolled a couple of times, finally coming to a sudden halt, courtesy of the curb. I laid there, the breath in my lungs sucked completely out of me.

Perfect execution once again, I thought, as I struggled to regain use of my now crumpled legs and arms. Nothing seemed to be broken. I felt a warm stream trickle down my face. I touched my forehead and felt for the source. I picked a small shard of safety glass out of the wound.

That's going to hurt, I thought, just before I lost consciousness.

Chapter 10

I awoke to the dimmed lights of a room. I couldn't see anything but shadows and every time I moved, my head started pounding again. The only one of my five senses that checked in for active duty was my hearing. There were muffled voices in the distance, along with a very loud ringing.

I wondered if this was what death was like. Had I finally kept my appointment with the Grim Reaper?

If so, I was deeply disappointed. I wanted to see the light in the distance, hear the trumpets blaring to announce my arrival, greet St. Peter at the gate, and best of all, watch my life flash before my eyes.

Damn! I really wanted that in-flight movie. Even in death I had been gypped. Can't someone give me a break here?

And then, suddenly, I was at peace. I wondered if I even had the chance to go to heaven, given my sordid past and my chosen profession. If only I had known I was going to die. I wouldn't have pummeled Steve's face into the table or made Jimbo pee his pants.

I tried to get up off the couch I was on. But it was no use. The pain was excruciating. There was no getting out of this one.

After what seemed like an eternity, someone finally

entered the room. I really hoped it was a friend not foe, for I wasn't exactly in fighting shape. I felt for my gun but it was gone, as was the holster. All that was left was a Redhawk-shaped bruise under my arm, a painful reminder that I had come very close to being road kill.

"Hey, boss, I see you finally came to."

It was Finchley. Thank god he had found me.

"Finch," I said slowly. "I have never been more glad to see you."

"You too, McCabe. That was a close call, wasn't it? I thought you had had it."

"So did I, my friend. But how did you know where I was?"

"Remember? You asked me to meet you at the office. I was running way early so I decided to practice my shadowing skills. I saw your car outside the Lazy Susan."

"Did you see who hit me, Finch?"

"Well, uh..."

"I'm just glad I didn't end up at the house of the crazy bastard who hit me."

"You did," Finch replied.

"Where are we?"

"Um, well... my house."

"You hit me?"

"Yeah, boss. Funny how it happened, too. As I said, I was practicing my tailing skills. I didn't have any real suspects so I thought hey, why not follow you for a while. Anyway, I saw you come out of the club and make your way across the parking lot."

"Go on."

"Well, what happened next is kind of fuzzy. It all happened so quickly. But my accelerator has been sticking lately and..."

"And?"

"You were one of the latelys," he said. "Man, am I lucky."

"You. Lucky. How?"

"I could have hit a complete stranger. Think of the chances of hitting your best friend instead. Sometimes things just work out in your favor."

If I had had an ounce of strength I would have killed him right there and then.

"So, let me get this straight. Last night you ran me over..."

"Oh, not last night, boss. It was Tuesday. A couple days ago now. You've been out a while. Today's Friday."

Things were rapidly going from bad to worse. Not only had my best friend almost killed me with that Crapillac he drives, but I had lost a couple days in my search for Lola's murderer. The killer was still on the loose and had at least a three-day jump on me.

My only hope was that he didn't know that I was on his trail. Hopefully, no one I had met tipped him off inadvertently, or worse, intentionally.

"Such good news, eh?" said Finchley.

"What good news, Finch? I hurt from one end to the

other, my best friend hit me with his quirky car and a killer is out there somewhere, either thinking he got away with murder or planning to commit yet another one. How is any of that good?"

"Well, uh, I have a $250 deductible and my insurance company says this is all covered. The doctor says you'll be just fine and oh, Melissa stopped by to see you."

Melissa? Why would she want to see me? I know the check was good. Did she want to go to the well again and add to her cause's kitty?

Obviously, I wasn't in any shape to see her.

"What did you tell her, Finchley? Did she leave a message?"

"Yup. She said that you'll want to call her. She remembered something else about that Darryl guy you were looking into."

I was hardly what I would consider presentable right now. Even the painkillers the doctor left behind weren't much help. Every muscle made a strenuous objection as I tried to move, alternately sending a shooting pain through my arms, legs and back like a pinball machine.

I asked Finchley to help me up. It took forever to get on my feet, but with Finch's help, I willed myself to the phone by the door. I pulled Melissa's card from my wallet and struggled to punch in the sequence of numbers that would connect me to her office.

She was out so I left a message. I knew that Melissa had something important to tell me. Otherwise she wouldn't have bothered to call me, let alone call on me.

Thankfully, Finchley had my car picked up at the Lazy Susan. Well, he didn't actually pick it up. His wasn't roadworthy after we kissed so passionately in the parking lot so he took the keys out of my pocket as I was taking my extended nap and drove me and my car to his house.

"Boss, you shouldn't be driving in your condition," he said. "Plus, you're on those painkillers."

"Finchley, if you'd read the bottle it says not to operate heavy equipment or farm machinery. My car isn't a John Deere. Besides, I've been in far worse shape than this."

"Well, boss, you ain't getting the keys. And for once, I'm in a position to be able to kick your ass. Not that my car didn't do a pretty good job of that already."

I wasn't exactly able to argue with him on that point. I was still in a lot of pain. I felt like I had been hit by a linebacker for the Seahawks. Blindsided, no less.

"Well then," I said. "Time for you to play chauffeur."

"Where we going, McCabe?"

"To visit an old friend, Finch. A very old friend."

As we made our way across town, I must have dozed off. Well, passed out is more likely. I had taken a double shot of pain pills washed down with a bottle of Rainier Ale, 'green death' as the locals liked to call it.

I groggily came to as the car came to a stop.

"Where are we?"

"West side of Lake Union. Roughly the middle of

nowhere. I thought you were going to see an old friend. But this address doesn't make any sense."

"To you, maybe. To me it makes perfect sense."

I climbed out of the Monster and told Finchley to meet me in an hour.

Even in my greatly reduced state, I easily found my bearings. To anyone else, the houseboats that lined Lake Union is a maze of floating homes, a hodge-podge of domiciles, some absolutely stately, others on the verge of sinking. The city had vowed to clean up this floating neighborhood in the name of urban renewal. But Seattleites hold onto the strangest traditions, and these houseboats, like the Twin Teepees on Aurora or the annual Seafair celebration each summer, were part of what made Seattle the biggest small town in the civilized world.

I made my way down the gangway that led to the interconnected finger piers that formed the streets of this part of town. A newcomer could easily get lost here and that was part of the plan. Sure, the residents could have gated the entrances, but there was really no need. As there was never any centralized planning, residents just kept expanding the neighborhood, tying up to another houseboat, dropping a finger pier between them and roping it to one of the existing planked thoroughfares.

If you wanted to navigate it successfully, you had to have been invited. Otherwise, you'd walk around for hours trying to find so and so's house, as none of the houseboats had addresses.

Well, not addresses that landlubbers were used to. Instead, you'd follow a long list of landmarks, turning right at the house with the two portholes, left at the two-story with the red door, then two rights beyond the piling with the pelican carving on the top, a left then a right and another left, the one by the converted tugboat.

That was my destination. It was owned by a dear friend of mine. Actually, he was the one who had gotten me into the private eye business in the first place. You could say he was my mentor, but that word doesn't fully describe him.

He was a surrogate father to me as much as my mentor, a great friend who had not only taught me about being a dick, but about life, too.

My own father had passed away years ago. He had literally worked himself to death. A self-made man, my dad hadn't made much of himself as a TV repairman. He thought the joys of working for himself would pay off big down the road.

They didn't. Instead, he discovered that being your own boss wasn't the panacea it was supposed to be. His days were filled with odd jobs that clients would pay him a pittance to do, if they paid him at all.

He slowly sank into a life of "wish I hads," sharing his dreams with the booze bottles he hid everywhere, trying to conceal this secret love from those closest to him.

I had to laugh. In many ways, I had become my father. I too had given up a promising career on the police force, thinking that I could do it better out on my own.

Call my own shots, "The sky's the limit," I would tell

myself, only to find that it often rained doom and gloom instead.

I never made it big like I thought. Still, I tried to convince myself that it could happen any day now. "This is going to be the case that makes me famous," I would think, only to find that it not only didn't make me famous, but it didn't make me a dime either.

I never wanted to be like my father. Growing up, I had seen what it had done to him. Being his own man had almost cost him his marriage.

My dreams of going to college vanished in the years following his death. My mother couldn't afford to send me to college. She had a hard enough time trying to feed me.

Instead, I ended up joining the local constabulary. I became a police officer in Renton. It was there that I met Sarge. His real name was Bill, but everyone referred to him by the nickname he had gotten while still walking the beat in Renton.

Sarge and I didn't get along well in the beginning. I was young and rough around the edges. Sarge had been tested by the passage of time; he was softer, more introspective.

Surprising, given that he was Irish to the core. Belfast born, and even though he had been in the states for more than 30 years, he still could turn on his rich Irish brogue whenever it suited him.

He had traded in his street-beat stripes by the time I met him and moved into the detective squad with the Renton force. He had a penchant for solving tough crimes, the ones that no one else could solve.

We worked together for the first time on the Ryan case. It was a difficult one for me as I had gone to school with the girl and we had dated a couple times. She was the victim of a grisly murder down by the Cedar River. A rafter had spotted her body floating face down near the train trestle, a stone's throw from police headquarters.

We knew that it was the work of a bold killer; professional grade.

It was Sarge who finally broke the case. The murderer had made one critical slip committing the crime. Forensics had missed the sliver of paint from a candy apple red Camaro during the autopsy, but Sarge had somehow spotted it under her fingernail. Like finding a needle in the proverbial haystack, for the paint chip was almost a perfect match to the candy apple red polish the Ryan girl was wearing at the time of the murder.

That's probably why the coroner missed it. I would say it was pure luck but Sarge was a very thorough investigator, always looking for that one clue that could break a case. He would review the evidence and the crime scene over and over again, never giving up.

I learned everything I knew from him – how to sweep a crime scene, how to look for the clues that always seemed to escape sloppy police work, and how to suspect everyone and anyone until the evidence pointed elsewhere.

It wasn't long before I made lieutenant with the force. I have Sarge to thank for that. We became fast friends and even in retirement we kept in regular touch.

"Well, if it isn't the Ace Private Eye himself," he said

as he opened the cabin door. "What brings you to my little seaside villa here?"

"Got a tough case, Sarge. I thought you'd like to put that mind of yours to work again and solve something besides a crossword puzzle. If you can handle it."

"Handle it, my ass, McCabe," he said, opening the screen door. "The mind is sharp as ever, even if these brittle bones aren't as spry as they used to be."

He made his way over to the sofa and sat down, his cane leaning on the armrest.

I sat across from him. The Lay-Z-Boy had definitely seen better days, tattered and torn from years of use.

"Wanna beer, boy?" he said.

"No thanks, Sarge. Had more than a few a while ago tending to an occupational hazard."

"Hazard, huh? Finchley, I presume?"

"You never miss a thing, do you Sarge?"

"Well, it's one beer then. Go ahead, make yourself useful and get it for me. Hurry up, too. This thirst isn't going to quench itself."

I struggled to my feet as best I could, answering his request like I used to answer his orders in the field. Some habits are hard to break.

I grabbed two beers from the fridge. I knew Sarge didn't like to drink alone and if I came back with only one, he'd continue to guilt me until I caved.

"So, let's hear your little tale, McCabe. It has to be a doozy to bring you all the way down here."

I recounted the case of Lola's murder. The visit by her

refrigerator-sized boyfriend, the finger lickin' chicken friend, the encounters with Melissa and Darla, and the occupational hazard, my run-in with Finchley.

"I was wondering why you were moving so slow, son. I thought you were starting to get old on me."

"Here's the problem, Sarge," I said. "I'm not seeing any patterns here. There seems to be no motive. Lola seems to have been well liked. She didn't have any enemies, at least any I can find. All I have is an odd picnic photo, a couple of loose connections and a dead body."

"Let me see the photo."

I handed him the photo from the lab. He peered at it for a moment, then got a twinkle in his eye. "Who's the hot chick in the front?"

"That's the victim, Lola Chase."

"Man she's hot. Or should I say, she was hot. Probably looks a bit like Gainsborough's Blue Boy now. But a hotter version of it."

"Geez, Sarge, have some respect for the dead here. For cryin' out loud."

"Had the hots for her, did ya, boy?" he said. "I can see it in your eyes. You shouldn't really be on this case. You know how having a connection to the deceased can mess up your mind. You remember the Ryan murder."

"Of course I do."

"Didn't you have a thing for her in school? Wasn't she going to be a future-ex of yours at one point? Your 'one true love' if I recall?"

"Yeah, what of it?"

Sarge leaned forward, looking right into my eyes. He let the moments slide by, like he was fishing and was about to set the hook."

"Nothin'. Nothin' at all," he said, taking a last swig of his beer. "Fetch me another one of these, McCabe. The day's slipping right by. I haven't gotten a buzz yet and it's damned near 11:30."

Dutifully, I got up again and headed back to the kitchen. I took the last beer out of the fridge and handed it to Sarge.

"Here you go, you old fart. Now tell me, what's on your mind."

"First, McCabe, you seem to have a quirky thing for blonds. Remember that girl? The rich one… what was her name again?"

"That was Melissa."

"Melissa. Wait. The same Melissa in the tale you just told me?" he said. "Geez, McCabe. You know, there are lots of women of color who are solid dating material."

"You mean blacks and Asians?"

"Hell, no McCabe! I'm talking about redheads and brunettes… get your head out of your ass and try a different color for a change. It will blow your mind."

"And hey, I don't think Melissa really counts," I countered. "I mean, does hair color really count when you're doing the mambo in the sack and the lights are off?"

"You mean – "

"Yup, she was my 'lights off' girl."

"You sly dog, McCabe. I didn't think you ever did the big nasty with Melissa. She wasn't a 10 in the looks department but hey, I'd do her."

"In the dark," we both said at the same time, laughing.

"What she doesn't make up in looks she makes up in the sack, Sarge, let me tell you. A real wildcat when she's off leash. And man, she had some major construction since – she's a total babe now. But let's save the details for another time. I really need help with the Chase murder."

"McCabe, you know better than I do. You need to question everything. Nothing is ever as it seems on the surface. You need to dig deeper. A silly picnic photo, a Jamaican bouncer and the sister of Chicken Lickin' isn't going to lead you anywhere. You need to find the connection.

"Personally, I think your dick is doing all the thinking here," he said, turning to watch a boat pass by on the lake. "You're not interested in finding the killer as much as you're interested in getting some revenge on the guy who offed the object of your erection."

He was right, of course. I was interested more in personal justice than the public kind. I really needed to rethink my priorities here and go back to being a dick without such a hard-on for the perp.

"Thanks as always Sarge," I said. "I get what you're saying. I need to go back to square one and retrace everything that's happened up until now. There has to be something I've been missing."

"Now that's the McCabe I know. And one more thing, McCabe. Don't take anything at face value. Even those closest to you may have something to hide. Remember what I told you?"

"Suspect everyone and anyone until the evidence points elsewhere," I said, glancing at the floor in embarrassment.

"You know as well as I do that being caught up in a crime can do funny things to people, even people you've known your entire life and who you trust with your life. Watch your back and realize that everyone could be tryin' to sell you something right now."

"Thanks for the advice, Sarge. At least I can trust Finchley, eh?"

"Can you?" he replied. "I said everyone McCabe. Even your dearest friend or your closest partner."

Chapter 11

As I walked back down the dock, I couldn't shake what the Sarge had said: "Even your dearest friend or your closest partner."

How could Finchley ever be involved in Lola's murder?

I shook the thought off. I just couldn't go there. Dutifully, Finchley was waiting in the marina parking lot. Well, he wasn't exactly waiting. Sleeping is more like it.

I jumped into the passenger side of the Monster. Still no reaction from Finchley. Thank god someone wasn't trying to kill *him*. They would have had to wake his sorry ass up just to get any enjoyment out of doing the deed.

I hit the horn on the Monster and Finchley sprang back to life, reaching for his gun, eyes wide as saucers.

"Sorry, McCabe. I didn't get much sleep after running you down."

"Guilt, perhaps?" I asked.

"Funny, boss. No, you snore like a freakin' lawnmower. One more pull and I could have done the lawn."

I could thank my grandfather for that. When I was a

child I marveled at his ability to keep an entire house awake with his snoring. It never woke him. I used to watch him take an afternoon nap, still wearing his white, short-sleeved dress shirt.

He snored with his mouth open, a perfect megaphone, one that hurled snores far and wide in a rhythmic style that bordered on hypnotic. I was sure he would start up like a lawnmower at some point and we could just take him out into the yard and cut the grass while he still caught a few more Zs.

We stopped at a nearby 7-11 so I could check messages. There was only one. My mother again, checking up on me.

She'd have to wait.

I thought Melissa would have called back by now. But there was no message. Strange.

I called her office. The receptionist said they hadn't seen Melissa since the night before and that her assistant was driving out to her house to check on her.

Not a good sign. Melissa didn't go incommunicado often. She was a slave to the office and to the technology that kept her connected to it and the world at large.

"Finch, we need to go – now!"

We shot back over to the Eastside as I continued to give weight to the advice that Sarge had given me. What was I missing? What were the dots of this case and how were they connecting? I couldn't see the big picture, perhaps clouded, as Sarge said, by that dumb dick of mine.

He was right in so many ways. Though I had tested the field over the years – mostly brunettes and brownettes – I did seem to have a thing for blonds.

Not bottle blonds mind you. Real blonds. I've had my share of the former and I'm not complaining. As one of my cop friends used to say, "Every chick you pass on is one less lay you're going to get in life."

I guess that's why I didn't put up too much of a fight with Darla. Well, that and the fact that she had me pinned to the floor, like throwing a sack of flour on top of an underfed rooster.

But a real blond? It's a rare bird these days. Finding someone whose blond window treatments match the carpeting can be a real challenge. There are a lot of smart hairdressers out there who can do the most amazing camouflage with hair, right down to the roots and even the brows. Speaking about bait and switch.

Someday I'll have a real blond in my life, one that isn't pushing up daisies.

As we pulled into the mansion drive, the policeman standing guard at the gate let me know that it wouldn't be Melissa, lights or no lights.

The coroner's wagon was there, as was Grist's car. My heart sank, knowing that Melissa didn't leave a message for a reason. She had been silenced.

I was met at the door by Grist.

"McCabe, why am I not surprised to see you here? Why don't you just leave the real police work to us? You seem to have this odd knack for showing up at murder scenes and I'm beginning to wonder if you're the cause of all this carnage."

He leaned against the doorway, blocking my entry.

"You seem to really have a way with women. They all seem to end up dead lately. But I can't help but wonder: Is it just odd coincidence or are they just taking the easy way out so they don't have to be the object of your misplaced affections."

I wanted to belt him right then and there, but doing even a day in the hokey-poke-me would lead nowhere, especially in my reduced state. I bit my tongue and chalked it up to Grist being jealous, figuring his Johnson hadn't seen a cave of delights since the Johnson administration. At least one that didn't charge admission.

There wasn't much I could do here. There was no way Grist was going to let me go past him. His broad stance on the stoop made that clear.

As I walked away, I couldn't help but wonder who would kill Melissa? Well, she was filthy rich. But who would gain from her death? She didn't have a husband, an ex, except me, of course, or any children. Besides, she would have most of her estate tied up in her work with the Helen Keller Foundation charity, Random Acts of Blindness.

Were Lola's and Melissa's deaths connected? Was Grist right in saying that maybe this was about me, not them? That someone was taking their revenge out on me by killing my friends?

But Melissa wasn't my friend, really. Just a passing ship in a sea of loneliness. And Lola was an unrequited love that few outside of Finchley knew about.

Finchley! Geez, could Sarge be right?

No, Finchley couldn't be blamed for much of anything, except being two feet short of a yard and not knowing the difference between an accelerator and a brake.

I could easily take him off the list of suspects. At least for the moment. Still, Sarge's words haunted me.

I got back into the car, silent.

For once, Finchley didn't say a word. He simply backed the Monster back down the drive, took out part of the hedges, bumped into what I would assume was a prohibitively expensive urn and drove off as it crashed loudly to the pavement.

"Where to, boss?" he said after a moment or two.

"I have no idea, Finch, old friend. For once I am just like you, clueless."

Not having anywhere else to go, we returned to the office. Every usually painful step up the stairwell was all the worse with the various bumps and bruises I had from my earlier run-in with Finchley's car.

I jostled the keys in the lock, but the door swung open on its own. Someone had been here already. Finchley drew his weapon as I swept the room with my keen private eyes.

Then, a noise from the corner of the room. Instinctively, Finchley shot at it. The once gurgling water cooler exploded in a furious spray, covering the walls and floor.

"Sorry McCabe. I guess I forgot to lock the door when I left yesterday."

Thankfully, the water cooler company was on my "to pay" list, a couple notches below power and phone.

"Finchley, I think I had enough of you today. Uh, I mean, I think you've had enough for today. I'm going to stay here at the office for a while."

"No prob, I'll be happy to keep you company," Finch replied.

"I think you're missing a cylinder or two here, Finch old boy. I want to be alone with my thoughts."

As the light bulb finally flickered in Finchley's head and almost went on for a moment, he decided he should leave.

"See ya later then, boss. Here are the keys to the Monster in case you need them. I'll just walk home."

As Finchley closed the door behind him, I wondered how long it would be before he realized that he moved out of that walkup he had in the International District and had moved to the 'burbs.

I didn't give his upcoming journey much more than a passing thought before I retreated into my own head to consider the events that had transpired over the last two weeks.

I was still haunted by the thought of Melissa's last moments. I had no idea how she died. Maybe she chanced upon an old photo of herself and was scared to death.

I know, kind of a shitty thing to say about a stiff you once shagged. But gallows humor has always been a way for me to keep an even keel in life, balancing the horrors of the daily grind with a little humor.

I didn't really mean anything by it. After all, Melissa and I had been intimate a time or two or three or four. Now she was gone. I guessed that I was still in shock, this doubling down on the dead in my life. Most of the cases I had been brought in on involved total strangers. I was arm's length from their lives, so I didn't have to feel much. It's something a private eye can't afford to do – leave himself open to feeling something.

And yet, here I was, immersed in a double homicide; one, someone I adored from afar, the other, someone I had once danced with between the sheets.

My mind was cloudy with a slight chance of brain. I needed to do something to clear my mind, or at least give me a good reason to be partly cloudy.

For once, booze wouldn't be the salve that soothed my open emotional wounds. I just couldn't go there right now.

Instead, I opted to take the short walk to Umbertos, a quite little Italian bistro in Pioneer Square. It was my kind of place. Not as divey as I like, but the waiters were just as self-absorbed and rude as those at Dirk's or the Dog House. For some reason, it felt like home. Not Umbertos necessarily, just the "who gives a shit you're here" atmosphere of a place with some filling food and "so-so, you're lucky I stopped by your table" service. It was like eating at my mom's house.

Such was Umbertos. The main advantage of the place: It wasn't Dirk's, yet I could still walk there, albeit slowly and with something of a gimp.

I carefully made my way down the stairs that led to the café below ground. It was in what would have been part of the Seattle Underground, which was created when much of the city burned down at the turn of the century and was rebuilt one level up from what was once the main street. Today it's a tourist attraction for the city. I knew the underground well, not from the tours but from my vocation. There were times when I had to go underground, literally, and the passageways of Seattle's past created the perfect place to hide out for a while.

As I made my way into Umbertos, one waiter rushed by me, opening the door I had just come through. Another, along with the owner, was dragging a pirate down the hallway. He had obviously seen better days, passed out now and by the looks of him, had lost at least a carafe of wine in the restroom.

Pirates are one of the quirky things about living in Seattle. No, Seattle had never had any real pirates. Blackbeard, Morgan and the likes were too smart to come this way, preferring the lucrative waters of the Caribbean to the frigid waters of the Puget Sound.

Instead, the city had play pirates. Every year during the Seafair celebration, they landed by way of a World War II landing craft on Alki Beach, stole away with a couple of festival princesses, loaded them onto their rolling dumpster of a parade vehicle, and roamed the streets for a couple weeks, appearing in parades and raiding bars.

The only thing they didn't do was grow up. I had only run into them a time or two at the Dog House, one of their favorite haunts. It had at one time been owned by a Seattle Seafair Pirate, so they could get away with their antics and womanizing there and no one would look twice.

By the looks of this lone pirate, I could see that the group had seen better days. He was a mess and I actually felt bad for the wait staff that had to drag him out of the bathroom and eighty-six him from the restaurant. I can't even imagine what the restroom looked like.

It didn't take long to find out, however. The pain meds seemed to have freaked out my bladder. I felt like I was pregnant, about to burst, even though I had just gone to the john at the office.

I went back to the restroom, opening the door with more than a little dread. My prediction was spot on. The poor lad had lost it in the urinal, in the sink, on the floor and in the toilet stall. Red wine and oysters covered the entire space – it looked like a murder scene.

I backed out just as the dishwasher was rolling in a bucket and a mop. Poor guy.

I would have continued to feel sorry for him but I had a more immediate need at hand. As I pushed on the door to the woman's restroom, it offered no resistance. A very comely woman was just leaving.

I greeted her and then noticed the "I've Been Had By the Seafair Pirates" button that had been secured to the peak of her breast, as if the pirate who had pinned it on her had Robin Hood level accuracy for hitting the bullseye.

Well, he wasn't alone, at least. I wondered why such a beauty could take up with such a drunken lout, but then checked myself, as he and I weren't really that much different in that respect. No calling the kettle black this time.

As she sashayed away, I laughed to myself that she had indeed been had or soon would be, as I'm sure he didn't pay the bill before he was drug out of the place and tossed onto the sidewalk above.

I did the task at hand and returned to the dining room. It took a few minutes to be seated, even though there were only three other people in the cafe, the young lady who was getting her first look at the pirate's tab and a couple obviously on their first date, a stilted conversation marked by awkward moments of complete silence.

I sat down and looked through the menu. I really needed a pick me up, so I ordered the Eggs Purgatory, an egg poached in marinara, served with brioche over a pile of hash browns.

Thank god they invented credit cards. They allowed me to live way beyond my means, even though my means were meager at best. Still, the float on the credit cards allowed me to up the ante on my meals, giving my gullet a break from the cleansing power of the fare at Dirk's Diner.

I didn't wait long for Purgatory. As my meal arrived the now pirate-less lass departed, looking a bit disappointed, perhaps because she, not he, got stuck with the bill.

As I ate, I thought again about Melissa's last moments here on this earth and then, whether or not there was any connection between her death and Lola's.

Tummy pleased, I headed back to the office. I stretched out on the couch, covered my face with my fedora and drifted off to sleep, knowing that the murder would be front-page news in the morning. The Post Intelligencer had a reputation for yellow journalism and I knew that the death of a prominent millionairess would automatically become the day's top headline, with every gruesome detail spelled out.

I awoke from my exhausted stupor still on the couch. I wasn't surprised that I had fallen asleep, given the painkillers and full stomach. I stretched a bit, a sharp reminder that I was still on the mend.

True to form, the paperboy had slid a copy of the PI under my door. I rose slowly and awkwardly from the couch. I should have just crawled; it would have been much easier and far less painful.

Above the fold, the headline said it all:

MILLIONAIRESS MURDERED

A photo of Melissa at her last charity function was placed to the right of the story that told the gory tale of her demise. According to the story, she was found in her bedroom by her assistant. No pulse. No apparent signs of forced entry. Police were still looking for leads, including looking at surveillance footage of the home and its approaches. The coroner was conducting the autopsy but results wouldn't be available for at least a couple days, if not a week.

I wondered how I would be able to get the autopsy repor...

Geez! The autopsy report. Finchley had purloined a copy of Lola's report but I had totally forgotten about it. Being hit by your friend's car and having a former friend with benefits offed can make you forget a few things. But the autopsy report? How could I let that slip my mind?

I returned to my desk and called Finchley.

"Finch?" I said. "Get down here quick and bring the report with you."

"What report?" he replied.

"The autopsy report, Finch. Geez, do I have to remember everything?"

Obviously, I did.

Chapter 12

As I awaited Finchley's arrival, I poured over all the clues and dead ends I had come across in the last few weeks. Nothing was adding up, particularly the numbers in my bank account, which was dwindling by the day as I pursued Lola's killer without a thought to my business.

Speaking of dead ends. This was one case that would never pay off. Lola was a goner and my FWBM (friends with benefits millionaire) was dead now, too. Exes were stacking up like cordwood that no one wanted to foot the bill for.

I doubted Bubba would pony up any cash to cover my expenses. He hardly had what anyone could call steady income. And Sarge, well, we were best of friends but being Irish, he would squeeze a penny until Lincoln cried out in anguish. Plus, he made it a policy never to lend money to friends.

Besides, who would be fool enough to front funds to a private eye? It wasn't like we were a good credit risk, given that crime, at least when it comes to being a private eye, definitely does not pay.

To kill time, I went through the bills that were in various stages of overdue. I hadn't even bothered to open the stack, knowing that there was little to no point, given that my bank account was headed south faster than Amtrak's weekly runs to Los Angeles.

Los Angeles. Now there's a place where even the worst of private eyes could make a good living. There were enough tawdry affairs in Hollywood to keep a guy busy day and night, knowing that the alimony alone would yield a healthy paycheck from a broken-hearted starlet whose private life made headlines in the Enquirer. Add in the hush money from the studios that wanted to keep their dashing, leading man out of the papers and you could easily make bank in LA.

In Seattle? Compared to LA, the people of the Northwest were squeaky clean. No one really cares who is sharing sheets in Seattle as there is a certain societal code that people, decent people, don't talk about such things, except perhaps over a rousing game of canasta and a glass of wine.

And really, who would care about any indiscretions in Seattle? No one famous really lives here. They all move to LA or New York once they strike it big. Just look at Bing Crosby and Kenny G. They hightailed it out of Seattle because it's just a little too quaint, a little too small town, for anyone truly famous.

Soles greeting the squeaky steps of the stairwell let me know I soon would have company. It's about time that Finchley got his butt down here.

"Finch... what took you so..."

It wasn't Finchley. The Incredible Bulk had returned. I thought Bubba and I had finished our business, but for some reason, he thought a second visit was warranted.

"McCabe, mon." he bellowed as he walked through

the door. "Mind if I come in?"

"Seems like you already are in, Bubba. What can I do for you?"

"I think someone is following me, McCabe," he said. "I don't know if it's just me being a bit paranoid or if someone's out to get me."

"Go on."

"You know me, McCabe. I am an entrepreneur of sorts. I have my hands in a lot of revenue streams…"

"Yes, I know, Bubba."

"I know how to give someone the shake. And I know how to blend in if I need to."

I let go a laugh, given that there no street post or tree on this planet could possibly hide his fat ass. The extra-large pink Hawaiian shirt alone would make hiding a difficult undertaking, even in a dark room.

"What you laughin' about McCabe," he said, rising from his chair. "I don't find anything funny about being followed morning, noon and night."

Just as he was about to practice pretzel-making with my wiry frame, Finchley came through the door.

"Hey boss, I brought you the autopsy…"

Bubba dropped the hold he had on my necktie and turned to face Finchley.

"You!" he said. "You're the one."

In one fluid motion, Finchley turned tail, dropping the report on the floor, papers scattering about as he made for the stairs.

Bubba huffed, then puffed, but he did not blow the

office down. Instead, he took after Finchley, as if he was a heat-seeking missile that had locked onto its target.

As Finchley scampered down the steps two, three at a time, I marveled at how fast Bubba could move for such a large man. Must be all that practice he got with the police; he the prey, not the hunter.

I thought about engaging in the chase but figured that with any luck Bubba would catch Finchley and even some of the scores I wished I could settle with him. Dammit, you just can't really pummel your best friend; at least one that already has big trust issues.

Oh, well. I've gone it alone before. With any luck Finchley would duck down the alley I always use to evade the landlord and his ever-present eviction notice. It works like a charm, at least for me.

As Finchley ran for his very life, I picked up the papers from the floor, restacked them and returned to my desk.

I've seen more than my share of autopsy reports, that's for sure. But never have I had to pour through one that spelled out in graphic detail how an object of my affection had been murdered.

I briefly scanned the description of her body in the morgue. I'd already seen it up close and personal and nothing in that part of the report would be any help. I continued to turn the pages, reading through toxicology and then into the actual dissection and the coroner's notes.

Asphyxiation. It isn't pretty. Humans don't like it

when they can't breathe. Even when it's accidental, there are signs that the body is trying its damndest to get enough oxygen to stay alive. There are often signs of a struggle, such as the inhalation of some of the materials surrounding the person – mud, grain, coal dust or sand. It shows up in the lungs or even on the victim's mouth.

If Lola had been a hostage and confined to a small space when she died, there would be signs of CO_2 or other gases in her system, replacing the oxygen she would have liked to have been breathing instead. None. No sign of high levels of nitrogen either, so she didn't go for a ride high in the sky or down in the briny deep before she bought it.

Nothing was really odd or out of order. She had some slight bruising around her mouth and nose, but no lacerations. There was also some bruising on her chest and she had a few cracked ribs, which was a bit strange, since there was no skin residue under her nails or any other physical signs of a struggle.

No signs of drugs in her system either. Just a low level of Ambien, a new favorite in the doc-in-the-box world for treating sleep disorders. The cops in Seattle were being kept on their toes with this new drug, as slight overdoses would cause sleepwalking, personality disorders and a feeling of drunkenness. More than one driver ended up in the tank overnight, booked on suspicion of dabbling in too much Ambien after blowing a big goose egg on the breathalyzer.

A good dose of Ambien would have given her a splitting headache in the morning to be sure, but it wouldn't have been enough for a one-way ticket to see the Reaper.

Finchley had finished his workout with Bubba and returned to the office.

"Whew... boss... I... thought... I... was a.... goner."

"Why did he chase you like that, Finchley? Did you do anything I should, you know, know about?"

"I was following him now and then. I wanted to see if he knew more than he was letting on, or consorting with someone who could help us crack this case wide open."

I definitely wanted to crack a case all right... but with my bank account heading to hell in a hand basket, it would have to be a case of Rainier and not the bourbon I craved.

But there would be plenty of time for that later. I needed to have a clear head and I needed to keep as many of my brain cells alive as possible, at least for now. There would be plenty of time to put their lives on the line somewhere down the line.

I gave my partner the highlights of the autopsy report. Then we went over the police report, the final one.

Yes, she had been found in the reeds by Duck Lake. The jogger said she could see Lola's legs sticking out slightly as she went for her run on that fateful morning, the reeds bent in a rough body shape as her expired frame extended into the lake. She was still clothed, wearing a pair of Normandy Rose jeans, matching jean jacket and a pink crop top.

No sign of struggle at the crime scene. Strange. You'd think that you'd fight for your life if someone was trying to strangle you. The surrounding area would be disturbed more. The photos did show some additional bending and breaking of the reeds, but that could jibe with someone dragging her into the reeds and posing the body in its final resting place.

But there was no telltale set of footprints heading into and out of the actual crime scene. Oh, sure, there were footprints aplenty around the crime scene. Little feet making mad dashes to the water; larger ones making equally mad dashes to keep them out of it; and the solitary ones of fathers pretending to dutifully watch the stroller, picnic basket or whatever they could think of, all the time wondering if the kid was really theirs.

Geez, what happened to the days when people planned their families and just didn't roll the old baby-making dice after a night of cheap liquor and equally cheap sex? I've heard the "Oh, honey, don't worry, I'm using protection" ruse all too often as I did some of my less stellar private eye work when I was just starting out and I'd end up doing a little sexveillance on the side. Amazing what a hidden mike and a Radio Shack tape recorder can get you.

Thankfully, I had no need to worry about such things, at least for the foreseeable future. A private eye who can barely pay for a cup of coffee, let alone a real date, isn't exactly a babe magnet. True, I wasn't too bad in the looks department. I could hold my own in the sack. But the lack of a bulge in my pants was a real turnoff to most women, and no, I'm not talking about the one in the front, but the one in the back.

A lot of ladies are attracted to a fat wallet. I guess that's what made Lola such a catch in my eyes. She didn't really seem to care if I had any flow in the dough department. We connected on so many other levels.

O.K., so we never had the chance to connect at any level. We never actually dated, so I would never know what would have happened when the check came and I looked off in the distance, as if thinking about the tip I should leave.

That trick has actually worked a time or two. You look off for a bit, then glance at the check, talk some more, mention that you hoped a couple of your clients came through in the payment department, excuse yourself briefly to go to the bathroom – seeing if it's possible to give the hostess the bum's rush and dash out the door – then return to the table when that didn't work and if your date hadn't already reluctantly paid the check, ask her if she can spot you a couple bucks until Friday and make sure you never call her again.

I never would have done that to Lola. A class chick, even in her current state. I'd like to think she would understand though, if I had. She'd just tap the mad money she always kept in her shoe and waltz me out the door to get her money back in the sack.

I really need to date more. Check that. I really need to date. More would be even better, but I would take just about any date right now, even Connie back at the TNT.

Now that's desperation. Maybe this preoccupation with my love life and its lack of a future with Lola gone has thrown me off the track. Maybe that's why my usually keen private eye instincts were so off the mark. I was consumed with doing the Hokey Poke-me with virtually anyone it would seem.

Man, I had to clear my head. The one on top of my neck. No matter how desperate I have ever been to get in a little lovin', I've never stooped to paying for a ride on the wild side.

First, I was not the type to hire a hooker. Sure, I've had my share of whores and bimbos, but only in a professional sense. Wait, that came out wrong in my head. Let's just say I was on the client's dime so hitting up a streetwalker up now and again was just part of the job. Geez, that didn't sound right either. Damn!

O.K., let's start over. Hookers, whores, bimbos and druggies are often a great source of information. They won't give it to you for free – the information – but they are, let's just say, out and about at odd hours on the job and see things as they are doing it.

Crap, I give up.

A second reason? Remember that bulge in my pants? The lack of it was a deal killer from the get-go. After pumping them for information and cashing out, there was very little wad left to shoot the other way. Hookers hardly wear a change maker around their waist, though that could actually be good for business. And slightly sexy. Cha-ching!

But once again I digress. Back to the case.

I left Finchley at the office, knowing that Bubba was probably still trolling the streets of Pioneer Square looking for him. It wouldn't dawn on him for some time that Finchley gave him the ol' sliparoo and doubled back to the office. I only hoped that he wouldn't be too quick to figure that out, or Finchley would end up a broken, broken man and I really couldn't afford to find another detective who would work with me for free.

The Monster knew the way. I'm glad it did. Often it would end up where I didn't even know I wanted to go. I'd just come out of some preoccupation I was consumed with and there I was, parked just where I wanted to be.

Maybe that's why I never sold the Monster. It was a love-hate relationship, true. My love affair with cars always is. Like horses, they hate me and I hate them. They have left me on the side of the road more than my dates. I can almost hear them laughing at me, mocking me in their sublime superiority. They knew I would have to fix them, no matter how much they sputtered spewed, coughed or wheezed, jerking to a stop on a busy highway or byway, as far away from home and a phone as they could get.

But the Monster? She was dependable. She only left me once, in a parking lot. I looked under the hood to see what was wrong, but I had no idea. I knew there was a motor in there somewhere, but that was the extent of it.

Thankfully, Sarge was a whiz with cars and the next day he came to my rescue. About an hour into the task at hand, he asked me to come with him. There, the Monster sat, the hood up, some mysterious tools resting gingerly on the fender, Sarge with a look of amusement and consternation.

He reached down into the bowels of the Monster, pulling something from its belly. He looked me straight in the eye, holding some foreign object in his hand.

"Do you know what this is?" he asked.

"Um, is this multiple choice? Or true and false?"

"Essay," he responded. "Take a wild guess."

"It has something to do with the engine," I hazarded. "It looks like it has, what do you call those?"

"Threads?" Sarge replied.

"Yes. That's it! So I assume it is screwed into something. The engine?"

"Geez, McCabe! The Monster deserves someone better than you as her owner. These are spark plugs. There are eight of them and they are in very, very sad shape. When did you change them last?"

"Uh, let's see. I bought the Monster when she was just two years old. So that was 1975. And it's what? 1985 now? So…"

"You've never changed them have you?" he replied, shaking his head. "See this?"

He showed me what I could only assume was an important part of the spark plug. It extended down below the threaded part.

"This is the electrode," he said. "It's what makes a spark in your engine."

"And the spark does…" I replied, trying to feign interest.

"For crying out loud McCabe! Didn't you ever take shop in high school?"

I hadn't, of course. One of my older brothers was a motor head so it became an instant turnoff for me. I went out of my way not to follow in his footsteps and now that decision was coming back to haunt me, at least at this very moment.

"The electrode creates the spark that ignites the gas in your engine that makes the cylinder go up and down which makes the..."

"Wheels go round and round?" I said proudly. "All over town?"

"Why do I bother with you when it comes to anything vaguely mechanical?" he said. "I would love to see your vacuum."

"I'd like you to see it too, Sarge. It sucks, but not in a good way right now."

"Never mind, McCabe," he said, a bit exasperated. He turned, looking back at the engine, a tool of some kind in his hand.

He went back to work. I was just glad he didn't hit me with the thing.

As I said, the Monster and I were great friends, even if it was something of a love-hate relationship. I could probably get another car, but none would be as faithful to me as the Monster. I can't even begin to tell you how many times she took me straight home from an otherwise debasing night of drinking my life away at the Benbow, Hattie's Hat or the Baranof. She knew the way home, taking me there when I could not, even stopping on occasion at Kettel's for some hangover fuel before dutifully guiding me back home.

The Monster dropped me off at the east parking lot near the concessions building. Once again, she knew the way, and once again, I didn't even know I wanted to go there.

I really didn't know what I would discover this time

at Green Lake. I had already surveyed the scene once, but something drew me back, and it wasn't the Twin Teepees on Aurora. Tempting ordinarily, but I really had bigger fish to fry.

Not that the fish in Green Lake were anything to write home about. But I wasn't here to fish, at least not in the classical sense.

Instead, I was fishing for clues, clues that perhaps the police had overlooked, if for no other reason than Seattle's detectives aren't exactly known for having a classical criminal mind.

Me? I tend to think like a criminal, even though I don't have a criminal bone in my body. Damn! If I had, then I wouldn't be here at Green Lake. Instead I'd be living on some tropical island down in the sunny Caribbean, occasionally visiting my money in the Cayman Islands, and in the interim, sipping on a tall, frothy blender drink with a 151 rum floater.

I could almost feel the tropical breeze, if it weren't for the unexpected rain shower that really should be expected when you live in Seattle.

There's an old joke about the weather in Seattle:

Who wrote The Bluest Skies You've Ever Seen Are In Seattle?

Answer: Helen Keller.

Still cracks me up.

Seattle weathermen could have a much easier time of their prognostications if they just said it was going to rain all the time. If it rains, great, you're spot on. If it doesn't, you're the freakin' hero for the day.

Why they would ever say it might be sunny is beyond me. Chances are, somewhere within the week you're going to be wrong and everyone is going to hate your guts, at least until the next time when it is actually sunny outside and you said it was going to rain.

I pulled the brim of my fedora down a little, trying to keep it from doing a Flying Nun and blowing back down the sidewalk in the now bustling, blustering breeze.

Fine time to take a walk, I thought. Especially since I was now halfway to my destination in a damned-if-you-do, damned-if-you-don't path back to my car.

It's not that I hated the rain. Having grown up in Washington, it's a part of you. The brief time I had spent in the Florida Keys and the always sunny days began to drive me a bit nuts. Maybe the sun was boiling my brain. But I really think that it's just part of being a Seattle guy – the rain gene gets in your DNA and you eventually miss it.

I began to wonder if it was misting or drizzling at the moment. Seattle people can tell and there is a difference. The Eskimos have some 50 words for the different types of snow, but no actual word for snow. Those who grew up in the Puget Sound region are a lot like the Eskimos. We don't really ever say it's raining. It can be drizzling, misting, pouring, piddling, pounding, pissing poodles, but never raining. There's no such thing.

Drizzle. Definitely drizzle, I thought. The misting had morphed unexpectedly; it was now a solid drizzle, And here it was just a mist a moment or two ago.

Thank god I owned a Fog. As I said, trench coats

aren't just a private eye stereotype; they really come in handy in the Northwest, protecting you, sheltering you and when necessary, keeping you from taking a pounding when the weather turns nasty, which it was beginning to be.

I thought briefly about making a mad dash for the car – just as the buckets began to spill from the heavens above – but I felt as if the ghost of Lola herself was guiding me back to the crime scene.

The police tape was long gone, of course, and the thickets of reeds had begun to spring back into their rightful place, but even so, it was impossible to miss the exact spot where Lola had died.

I knew there'd be nothing for me to find here. It's not that it was a grisly, blood spattered murder scene like some I've come upon. It was clinically clean and precise, as if she had been killed elsewhere and posed in the weeds.

Yes, that was still a possibility in my mind. Hollywood would like us all to think that depriving someone of air takes a couple of seconds. It doesn't. It's a very personal way to kill and the victim can hang on for up to five minutes before they finally succumb. If they're not willing to go easily, it can be a real fight to the finish line. It's not lot like being shot, which can come as quite a surprise. Before you are choked to death you usually know someone is trying to kill you and the fact that you like air, and a lot of it, can cause you to fight like a wildcat.

That's why I keep going back to the fact that Lola wasn't necessarily killed where she was discovered. As the autopsy showed, there weren't any real signs of a struggle and no water was found in her lungs, so the lake wasn't used to speed things up a bit.

Figuring I couldn't get much wetter than I already was, I stepped into the reeds. It took me by surprise. The lakebed sucked my feet into its ooze, like being stuck in muddy, mucky quicksand.

After a bit of a struggle, I finally freed my leg, but not without losing my loafer in the muck. Damn, this day was not turning out well at all.

I had little choice. I waded back to shore. I found a stick and plunged it into the muck, fishing for my shoe. Not wanting it to sink deeper, I was careful to guide the stick along the mud and muck at the same depth I thought my foot had sunk.

Pay dirt! I hit something hard so I started to ease it toward shore with my makeshift fishing pole. That was almost too easy, I thought, as I reached down into the water to retrieve my lost shoe.

I pulled it up, lost in a moment where expectations definitely didn't match reality.

Chapter 13

It was not my shoe.

Strange, I thought. I could understand why the forensics folks would have missed the shoe. You'd almost have to know it was down there or lost your own shoe and get lucky enough to pull this one up instead. Lucky me.

It was nothing that unusual as far as shoes go. I dipped it back into the lake so that I could wash the thick layer of mud off it, careful to hold it by the laces, just in case any prints could be lifted off the shoe itself. Doubtful, given its lengthy baptism, but I never liked to be sloppy in the way I conducted my work, at least not sloppier than usual.

The difference was like night and day. The shoe was a white leather Nike runner, the characteristic blue swoop running down its side.

Finally, something that might be a break in the case.

I couldn't easily tell if it was a man's or woman's shoe, the trend toward androgynous clothing and accessories spreading like a plague through the fashion world. Damn that Annie Hall.

I profess that I preferred the simpler times when a man looked like a man and a woman looked like a dame. High heels, short skirts and lots of bright red lipstick.

I set it down on the beach in the same position that I had pulled it out. I then went fishing again for my loafer. As I pulled the loafer from the muck I noticed something. It was pointing in a different direction than the Nike.

Who would lose a shoe like that? Even if they managed to keep the shoe on going into the water and lost it coming out, why wouldn't they retrieve it like I did? I mean Nikes aren't cheap shoes. You'd definitely want to spend a little time fishing for the one you lost.

Unless you didn't have the time.

Suppose the suspect lost the shoe while in the middle of committing the crime. He's in a hurry obviously, since he doesn't want to be discovered. He loses his shoe, decides to leave it behind, and flees the scene.

I heard a swishing-kersplashing on the lake, not far from where I was. I squatted down to stay hidden as best I could, unsure of who it might be.

A fisherman. How silly of me. As I said, the lake didn't have the best fish, but it was still fun to take a boat out and do a little catch and release. The bass and crappie were fun to fish for and the lake was perfect for fishing, especially since they outlawed power boats years ago.

By boat! That's how the murderer could have gotten in and out undetected. It would also explain why the shoe was facing into shore and not away. Why didn't I think of that earlier? Who's going to risk dragging a body across the grass from the parking lot? Even at night, someone could come upon the scene since Green Lake isn't exactly remote. There are houses, stores and bars all around it.

By boat. No one would think twice about someone out on the lake rowing a boat at any time of the day or night or any kind of weather. There were always a dozen or more boats out on the lake, piloted by fishermen or horny young men trying to score with their girlfriends, far away from the prying eyes of moms and dads back on shore who were too busy roasting dead animals and playing Frisbee to notice the carnal knowledge taking place just offshore.

Whoever did it could either hijack one of the rental boats or bring their own. The educated guess would be they brought one, loading it in down by the Aqua Theater, the body already in the boat under some tarps. If someone passed by, they wouldn't have a second thought about the fisherman heading out to do a little fishing, his stash of brewskis hidden under cover in case the cops strolled by.

To further reduce the chances of being discovered, he could have launched the boat later in the day and taken his time. Do a little pretend fishing while he waited for the perfect moment. As the sun went down he could row leisurely into the reeds and ditch the body in the shallows, making sure that she wouldn't drift back out into the lake, using her feet as an anchor on the shore. Once she was properly positioned, he could jump back up into the boat and take it back to the ramp. No one would have suspected a thing.

Except for the fact that he didn't know that during certain times of the year, the lakebed can get a little possessive, sucking your footwear right off your feet.

The murky waters, covered in a thick layer of milfoil, would make it nearly impossible to find anything stuck in the mud, especially when you're in a hurry to make a clean getaway.

I had a shoe, but where was Cinderfella? Seattle and its 'burbs was a lot of ground to cover, and it's not like a Nike is unusual around the Pacific Northwest, given that the region was filled with weekend warriors who actually thought running was healthy for them.

Hell, even I owned a pair of Nikes, much like the one I had in my hand. I never wore them, given my predisposition to falling in love with the idea of something.

I had done this many times in my life. I would readily fall in love with the idea of say, skiing. I would buy skis, bindings, bib overalls and head for the hills. I would try it a time or two, if I really liked it maybe a dozen times, then the icons of my "idea love" would be stored and forgotten, eventually given to a thrift store or left behind when I moved on.

That's how I came to own the running shoes. I was dating some dame at the time. It wasn't for very long, but she was a weekend warrior and thought it would be fun if we went jogging together along Alki.

I said, "Heck ya, I love running!"

What I was thinking was, "I love to *get laid*," but the word 'running' won the race to my vocal chords and slipped out instead.

Still hoping to get laid, I went to the mall and picked out a nice pair of running shoes – Nikes. I paid more than I should have but was hoping that after all those endorphins kicked in from running, we would want to do the big nasty to work out our collective aggression and energy.

We met at Alki. She warmed up a bit while I tried on the shoes for the first time. Off we went. Not 20 strides down the path and I was ready to die. The object of my affections was already a block away, looking back to see where I had gone.

I reached deep down and soldiered on. A man will do that when there's a woman he wants to sleep with. He'll damn near kill himself to show her that he's worth a toss or two under the sheets.

I swear we ran five miles that day. Since then I've come to find out that it was a little under a mile, an interminable half mile up and a grueling half mile back.

Afterwards, I feigned a little arch injury to gain some sympathy and to explain why I couldn't make it a mile without huffing and puffing.

She felt sorry for me, so much so that she took me to her place, slipped into something a little less comfortable, soothed my aching foot with a massage and made a play down under for some wonder, only to find that I had fallen fast asleep in her bed.

We never went out again.

The shoes? Well, they were now collecting dust in the back of my tiny closet, relegated to a life of waiting for the day when I would once again fall in love with the idea of running.

Trust me, that day will never come.

By now, the drizzle had let up and as I made my way back to the Monster, I passed a few very healthy looking gals starting their way around the lake. I momentarily thought about dusting off those Nikes, then thought better of it as I still had to find Cinderfella before he struck again, if indeed he had a plan to do so.

I popped the trunk of the Monster and pulled out a plastic bag for the shoe. I dropped it in and sealed it so that should the need arise, I could reclaim it in its current state.

I headed back to Pioneer Square, pulling into the alley behind the office and into the setback that served as the loading dock for the company next door. It was the weekend. There would be no deliveries today, or so I hoped.

I climbed up the flight of stairs. The lights were on in the office. Someone was home and it wasn't me.

I unsnapped the strap of my holster, just in case. The door slowly creaked open. Damn. I need to remember to grease that thing.

Lucky for me, no one was there for a change. It's hard to hide in my office – Lord knows I've tried on more than one occasion.

The only good spot had been under the desk, but the privacy panel had fallen off some time ago and not being particularly gifted in the carpentry or repair trades, I had never successfully put it back on. It had found a home, leaned up against the side of my desk, still in the same place where I had set it down just for a moment years ago.

Damn! Finchley must have left the lights on again.

How many times have I told him that I can barely afford the power bill when the lights were off, let alone all on. Even the desk lamp was a drain on my account, even though I had changed out the 75-watt bulb years ago for a 40.

You could say I'm cheap. I prefer to think of it as responsibly thrifty. Someday we'll end up with an energy crisis and I'm going to look downright visionary. But for now, I was suffering visionary problems of my own. The dim bulb, about as dim as my partner, had taken its toll on my eyes, making readers a necessary part of my life.

Few knew that I wore glasses. I probably should have seen an eye doctor about getting real glasses, but readers were cheap and disposable. Break a pair and a quick trip to Bartells would solve the problem. No need to lose an expensive pair of glasses while out on a case. It just seemed like an unnecessary expense, especially since reading isn't exactly a regular part of being a detective. Outside of the police reports, coroner reports, newspapers and menus at Dirk's or a comparable dive... O.K., so reading was part of the job.

Still, a couple pair of readers were doing the trick just fine for me and there was always a pair around somewhere.

Like the pair that just walked into my office. It was Darla.

"Well, what a surprise," I said. "Nice to see you again. I hope you're not back for sloppy seconds. I do my best work at night."

"In your dreams, McCabe. The first time was sloppy enough."

My ego retreated back into its small quarters near the exit sign of my brain.

"Fair enough. But I have to say, my heart wasn't in it."

"Neither was your pecker, McCabe. Neither was your…"

I cut her off before she could take another stab at my now winnowing sense of self.

She took her time waggling into the seat in front of me, her bosoms announcing every settling-in motion with an enthusiastic and obviously unrestrained swing from one side to the other in her scooping, tight blue sweater. It looked like the bells of St. Mary.

"What can I do you for then, if I'm not to do ya? Don't you have some, um, work to do?"

"Not for another couple hours," she said. "I swapped shifts with one of the other girls. I had to see you again."

"What was the rush?" I said.

"I'm worried about you, McCabe. I think you're holding on too tight to this whole Lola thing. I'm afraid you might make a mistake, that you're not keeping your heart and investigation separate."

"And why would this be of any concern to you, Darla dear?"

"Well, it's not really, I guess. Outside of the fact that you think my brother may be involved in this whole thing, though I'm sure he wasn't."

"And how would you know that?" I asked. "You've seen him lately?"

"Nope. He appears to have made himself pretty scarce."

"That's quite the challenge," I replied. "There can't be many places for him to hide, except the zoo. Most of him could hide behind an elephant, I would imagine."

"Cut the crap, Brewster. We're big people, we get it. It doesn't mean that we don't have the same feelings you do. Wait, strike that. It doesn't mean that we have feelings, as you obviously don't."

I admit that her direct nature was both refreshing and slightly sexy. I've always had a love of strong women no matter what size, shape or age. Though I hardly knew her, I found her intriguing to say the least, a woman so self-assured that she had no qualms about taking off all her clothes in front of men, leaving them with nothing but wet dreams. Except those she chose to entertain in her off hours.

"What makes you such a hard ass anyway, McCabe?" she asked. "Don't you ever have any feelings about anything?"

I did, of course. But showing one's emotions was a sign of weakness in the private eye game. I've seen the toll it can take on men in my profession. You leave your heart wide open and others waltz right in, taking what they wish and leaving nothing behind. Love and hate, joy and sorrow, they teeter-totter from one extreme to the other. Then, without notice, they hop off that teeter-totter of love and lust, leaving you to plunge to the ground, your breath taken from you along with all your pride and trust.

Far better to be a hard ass than to let emotions cloud your judgment. And yet, here I was, strangely attracted to a woman whose flesh and blood could be a cold-hearted murderer.

Darla got up to leave, largely because I couldn't give her what she wanted and she couldn't give me what I wanted.

"Just remember, McCabe," she said, as she turned at the door. "Everyone has someone, and amazingly enough, there really are those who care about you. Lord knows why they do, but they do."

She closed the door and left me there alone in my office and thoughts, my emotions teetering, then tottering, trying to make sense of this all too brief, and slightly strange, visit.

If only there was time for more self-indulgence. But I still had a killer on my hands and at least two victims hoping in the afterlife for vindication and justice. Indulging in my emotions wouldn't solve the case; it would only make things even more complicated than they already were. I really needed to clear my head and get back to work.

Unfortunately, there were few new clues. The shoe, of course. The fact that Lola may have known the murderer as there wasn't a huge sign of struggle or any marks on the body that would point to violence of any sort. There was the odd photo of Darryl at the picnic, the strange calls Lola got from the caller with a bad case of the munchies. Then, of course, was the fact that Darryl was still laying low, which either meant that he was a prime suspect or had no idea he was a suspect.

That would be hard to believe, given that his sister and I had had several encounters over the ensuing weeks. I really wanted to get my mitts on him so I could either finger him with Lola's murder or rule him out completely.

Chapter 14

Finchley had perfect timing. Notice I didn't say good timing. Instead, it was perfect: good, bad or otherwise.

This was one of those times. Though he missed Darla's dramatic exit, he could tell that something had struck me to the core.

"Somethin's up, McCabe," he said, as he sat down on the edge of my desk. "Now don't tell me. I'm a private eye, too."

I could almost hear his mind grinding along, searching for the cause of my malaise. Man that must hurt.

"Don't tax yourself, Finchley," I finally said. "I'll be fine."

His face continued to wrinkle and writhe as he searched for the answer. I let him take his time, knowing that it was part of the process of loading him back into the barrel of life.

Finally, his eyes brightened, at which point he replied, "Nothing. I've got nothin' boss."

I could have told him that.

I could see this little bonding fest was getting us nowhere. Somewhere out there a killer was on the loose and only he knew his next move. Unless...

I was about to take that to the next logical step when Finchley spoke up again.

"Geesh, where is my brain these days," he said. "I almost forgot that the police report came out on Melissa's murder. The coroner's still working on a final cause of death, but the report might be of interest to you."

"Ya think?" I said.

It was rhetorical at best. I wasn't really sure that Finchley did indeed think, except about the most basic things such as breathing and eating.

I opened the report and started to read through it. No sign of forced entry, nothing of value stolen, no witnesses. The staff was off that evening, including Melissa's personal assistant. Nothing appeared to be too out of order. The police had a look-see at the surveillance photo but it was grainy and dark.

I couldn't help but chuckle. While Melissa was known for her largess on many levels, she could also be something of a skinflint, a modern day Scrooge when it came to her own spending habits. Leave it to her to order a relatively cheap security system for a million dollar mansion, one that provided little to no useful information, just grainy shadows of nothingness.

If only she had ponied up a few more dimes for top-shelf equipment; we could have seen who had come and gone the night of her murder.

I looked at a few of the crime scene photos. Typical crime scene stuff. On the kitchen counter was a pizza, a slice and a half consumed, the rest left uneaten, the box top still open.

The pizza came from the Italian Spaghetti House. Strange, given that the restaurant was in Lake City and Melissa lived across the lake, far from the regular service area.

How did that pizza get all the way over there, I wondered.

I called the Italian Spaghetti House and asked to speak to the delivery manager.

After a few moments, he picked up the line.

"Italian Spaghetti House, would you like to place an order?"

"Do you deliver to the Medina area?" I asked.

"Why, sorry sir, we don't deliver to the eastside."

"Even for an extra fee?"

"Nope. Not that I've ever heard of. We don't have enough drivers to do a run out of the service area."

"Do you recall anyone calling to ask if you could do it for extra cash in the last two weeks?

"Nope. We log all the calls so that we can keep track of where our customers are and where a new restaurant might make sense. But no Medina calls."

"Thank you," I said. "I appreciate the information."

"Do you want to place an order anyway? For pickup perhaps?"

I hesitated at first, but then said, "Yes, a large Chef's Special, hold the anchovies."

I never could resist a good pizza. If there were only three foods in this world – pizza, burgers and almost anything from Taco Time – I could live forever.

Besides, when else can you write off a great pizza as a business expense? Yes, this was research. Important research. Well, at least that's what I will say to the IRS should I get audited.

Finchley and I headed down to the Monster. Thankfully, there had been no deliveries that day so it was right where I left her. We hopped on the Dearborn ramp and pointed the Monster north on I-5.

I hadn't been to the Spaghetti House in years, but had never forgotten that first bite of their delectable, delicious pizza. Crunchy crust, ooey-gooey cheese and plenty of meat, mushrooms and peppers.

"Finchley, here's a ten. Go in and pick up our order."

A moment or two later, Finch returned empty handed. "They didn't have a pizza under Finchley," he said, disappointed.

"You dolt. It would be under my name. McCabe. Remember? McCabe."

Finchley nodded as if this were some new information for him, then dutifully headed back into the Spaghetti House. A couple minutes later, he was back in the car, the piping hot pizza nestled between us in the front seat.

Finchley couldn't resist. He filched a piece of pizza as I checked the clock before pulling out of the lot. I headed back onto I-5, then took the 520 exit back across the lake. I took great care to go the speed limit, something I rarely do. Off the Clyde Hill exit, several more turns and finally, I was at the front gate of Melissa's.

I stopped the car and looked back down at the dash. Eighteen minutes had elapsed. Anyone could have delivered the pizza, but why would Melissa accept it if she had never ordered it?

That was a big duh! Who in their right mind would turn down an Italian Spaghetti House Special? It was legendary around here. All the driver would have to do is say that he got lost or that someone prank ordered the pizza and that he was going to get stuck with the cost if he couldn't sell it.

To make the sale, the delivery guy would open the top of the box and let the aroma of a fresh baked pie waft around the doorway a bit. Melissa would be dipping into her purse in no time at all.

Everyone's happy. Melissa gets one of the best pizzas in the greater Seattle area and the driver gets a victim.

But why Melissa? Why was she the target? Was it just a random act or was it planned all along?

It had to be the latter, if for no other reason than the killer chose irresistible bait – the pizza. No one at a pizza joint would think about someone ordering a pizza for takeout. Hundreds of people each week do just that with the Spaghetti House. It would be impossible to track back to the restaurant. They wouldn't remember who ordered what, let alone what they looked like.

But again, why her? It made no sense. Or did it?

I couldn't help but wonder if there was some connection between Lola and Melissa. I don't think they knew each other socially. I mean, Melissa wouldn't be caught dead at... sorry. She was hardly the type of person who would ever end up at Dirk's, even after an all night drunk. I don't even think she knew where the place was. And what could they possibly have in common?

Still, it had to be more than coincidence that a socialite and a waitress would be offed in a matter of days. I had to be missing something here. Perhaps the coroner's report would provide us with more clues.

"Finchley, can you use your connections again to get us Melissa's coroner's report?"

"I can give it the old college try, McCabe," he said anxiously. "Not sure how many times I can go to the well on that one, but I'll give it a shot."

I headed back across the lake, dropping Finchley at the office so he could pick up his car. I wheeled the Monster around in a quick U-turn and headed back home. It had been a long, long day. At least I could enjoy some pizza and a little boob tube before sawing logs.

When I awoke, I wasn't quite sure where I was or how I got there. It took me a few moments to figure out I was in my apartment. A good sign.

Then I noticed the piece of pizza resting quietly on my once fairly clean shirt. I must have fallen asleep a few minutes after I got in. I hadn't even made it through a single slice.

The pizza box was still next to me, the once hot pie now a congealed, cold mess of mozzarella, pepperoni, sausage, onions and peppers.

I slowly lifted the slice that passed out on my chest

from my shirt. Damn, that stain's never going to come out.

The thought of doing laundry was a frightful one. I tried to avoid it as much as possible. The downside of living in an apartment was the shared laundry room. Every time I tried to do my laundry, someone seemed to be using the machines. It's as if someone would hear me shepherding my dirty laundry towards the front door and make a made dash to the laundry, throwing in anything they were wearing or had within arm's reach – a single dish towel, a scanty piece of barely worn undies – just so I could experience the frustration of not being able to do my laundry – again!

Fortunately, I have learned to adapt with the times. I have several dozen tighty-whiteys in my dresser drawers, so weeks can go by without needing to wash anything, and if need be, I can squeeze through an entire month if I simply double up and change them on even numbered days. Or odd, if I felt like taking a walk on the wild side.

No point in even trying to wash the shirt. I was out of time and out of quarters.

I finished off my chest-piece and dove into another slice, then another from the box. I know there are some sissies out there who would never touch a pizza that had been out of the fridge all night. Well, in a man's world, whatever doesn't kill you makes you stronger, or sick. I'd find out in a couple hours what fate was in store for me. Me? I was rooting for the stronger option. Not because I'm some kind of macho whack job, but because I was out of toilet paper.

Until that moment of reckoning arrived, there was

work to do. A bit sore still from sleeping on my 20 piece erector-set sofa, I changed out of my shirt, took it and the rest of the pizza and put them in the trash can under the sink.

I rummaged through my pile of laundry on the bedroom floor and found another shirt, relatively clean, definitely rumpled, and changed into it after a brief man shower. Yes, a man shower. Splash some water on your face, spray some deodorant under your pits, dab on some Old Spice to cover up any additional and unknown fragrances, and head out the door.

All I knew as I headed out to my car was that I under-dosed a bit on the deodorant, for I could still catch a small whiff of stale pizza rising from my chest. Delightful. Maybe I shouldn't have been so hasty in throwing away the pizza. No matter. I could always retrieve it later when I got home, whenever that would be.

Hopefully, Finchley would have worked his magic and purloined the coroner's report on Melissa by now. I can't help but wonder sometimes how he manages to pull these things off. I made a mental note to ask him, though I am not sure I really wanted the answer.

Finch and I had arranged to meet at Dirk's in the morning. I was hardly hungry, given that I ended up sleeping with a Chef's Special. But a plan is a plan, especially when changing it meant the miracle of finding a way to leave each other a message to say that plans had changed.

Even if I stopped at a payphone there was no guarantee Finchley would be at the phone on the other end, waiting for a call. Sure, the answering machine was something of a blessing, but still, I longed for that day in the future when phones would no longer be tied together by endless lines of copper. My job would be much easier.

Sure enough, Finchley was in our usual booth, dutifully waiting for me to arrive. I felt a bit of sadness as I sat down, knowing that Lola wouldn't be our server today or any day.

"I got you a cup of coffee McCabe," Finchley said. "Thought you could use it."

I could, to lube the engine of the Monster. Dirk's coffee was famous, but not for any particularly good reason. Oh sure, I had had a latte or two in my time. Who hasn't, living in Seattle? It was tough to walk five blocks without running into a coffee shop or street corner stand hawking these legal highs.

I admit that I'm not much of a fan of anything from Starbucks. Their coffee of the day was always over-roasted and served so hot that you needed to wear thick winter gloves, even in the summer, to carry your cup. And those steamed milk drinks? What a nightmare. A couple bucks for a lot of milk and a small jolt of caffeine.

No, a regular old coffee, served black, did the trick just fine. But at Dirk's? Theirs was not for the faint of heart. They even had a sign out front that said proudly: "Our coffee is not for everyone, but everyone who is a fan, loves our coffee."

I was not a fan. But it would be a bit rude to walk in with a cup of coffee from another joint. You could probably get away with that elsewhere, but the waitresses at Dirk's Diner would definitely make life uncomfortable for you. It's been said that one gent ended up with his piping cup of Starbucks in his lap, his crotch burned beyond recognition, so much so that he had to ask the doctor for extra cream at the hospital. For the wound, not the coffee.

As Finchley's stack of flapjacks arrived, I decided to ask him about his talent for getting official documents that I could only dream of getting.

"Well boss, that's a very interesting question," he said, downing another wedge of pancake. "I can't help but be slightly amused by the fact that I seem to have a skill or two that you don't. You being more of a lady's man than I am."

"Lady?" I asked. "What lady?"

"Um, she works downtown," Finchley replied. "We've been seeing each other off and on for a couple months now."

"And?"

"Well, Angie has access to the coroner's office, being in the medical field."

"You're killing me, here Finchley," I said. "And I am warning you, I will not be the one to die here on this day, in this place, if you don't spill more details."

"O.K., O.K.," he said. "She's one of the nurses down there. You actually know her, nurse…"

"Cratchett?" I said, jumping to my feet. "You're boffing Nurse Cratchett?"

"Angie," Finchley said. "Her name is Angie and yes."

"Wow! And here I thought you had some kind of special connections."

"I do, McCabe. She's very special."

I couldn't help but wonder what Finchley could offer Cratchett or anyone else. But who says there's any logic in love? I was hardly an expert on the matter. I may have been in love with Melissa, I may not have been. I wanted to be in love with Lola, or at least a rousing state of lust. My other exes, well, I couldn't say I was ever really in love with any of them. At various times in my life I was more afraid of being alone than I was of giving into such a fickle and complex emotion as love. And really, who could love a guy who has a mistress – his work.

Not that my mistress was putting out at the moment.

But there was no way to fix that near term. My mistress would have to wait until I solved these two cases. I owed it to these two women, one a frisky bunkmate and the second an object of my affections, or at least, erections.

Finchley finished the last of his pancakes and picked up where he had left off.

"I should have the report by the end of tomorrow, McCabe. I'd have it sooner but Grist has been watching the place like a hawk. He's getting a lot of pressure from downtown now that Melissa is dead, too. He's been getting no help from the Bellevue detectives. He seems to think they are incompetent."

"He would know," I snickered. "He wrote the book on incompetence."

Finchley laughed, the last of his milk shooting from his nostrils. "You got that one right, McCabe. I bet he still has the signed first edition on his desk."

I flipped Finchley for the bill, made a big stink about losing the toss even though I didn't, then stopped at the counter to pay the bill. It was worth the couple of bucks it cost to feed Finch. Besides, he needed every dime he had to keep Nurse Cratchett happy, in and out of the sack.

Chapter 15

There wasn't much I could do until I got my hands on that report. After all, you can only circle around the same clues and the same locales so many times. While I was tempted to continue on my quest to find the killer, I didn't really have any new leads to work with. I was hoping the coroner's report would help in that regard.

I had almost forgotten what a day off looked like. I thought briefly about doing some shadow work for a couple of clients who wanted to see what their husbands were up to. But my heart wasn't in it. While it would bring in some much needed scratch, I could live off my credit card a bit longer; it hadn't found its limit quite yet.

I stood there in the parking lot, watching Finchley drive off. I'm not the kind of guy who has a lot of guy friends. Finchley was about as close as I got to a guy, well he and Sarge.

But these were professional relationships, not friendships. I could never see myself hanging out with either of them, going shopping or sharing stools in a bar, trying to lube up the ladies so we could divide and conquer them. That just wasn't my style.

For once I decided it wouldn't do me much good to hang out all day in a bar. Drinking alone and looping back and forth between the death of these two lovelies was hardly a great plan for the day. A *good* plan, yes.

But a *great* plan, no.

I could resurrect the pizza back at the apartment, but my apartment wasn't exactly the kind of place you wanted to hang out all day. It was more like one big storage unit with a bathroom, kitchen and windows. I had never even unpacked a lot of the boxes I had been toting from here to there over the years. There's only so much you need to actually live; the rest of it is just window dressing so that guests feel like they are visiting a home and not a storage facility.

Mine looked like a storage facility just the same. I didn't really have enough closet space to hide all the boxes, so they were just stacked about the rooms, one becoming an impromptu end table, another serving as a nightstand. Six others were stacked in the dining room, holding up a card table with a missing leg that I had found in the dumpster during moving day.

You know the day. At the end of every month, tens of thousands of people move from one place to another, and what doesn't fit in their truck or in their life ends up either next to or in the dumpster. For guys like me, it was a shopping bonanza.

I would like to say that my sofa and TV came from such expeditions, but they didn't. They were purchased at a neighborhood thrift store. The bed as well. I had always meant to purchase a bed frame for it. But I got used to it being on the floor. At least I never had to worry about being killed if I rolled out of bed wrong. A foot and a half drop couldn't hurt anyone.

I did, however, score a really nice steamer trunk and an Ethan Allen occasional table from the dumpsters by my house. These were real treasures of mine and had continued to make the cut when I was editing my house down to fit in yet another U-Haul.

Nope. Home was out.

Instead, I decided to go a very different route. I decided to head down to the Market. For those of you not in the know, the Market in Seattle is the Pike Place Market, but no one here calls it that.

Somehow, against all odds, the Market had evaded the wrecking ball and calls for urban renewal. The turn of the century mish-mash of vendor stalls, shops and sellers who hawked everything from fresh flowers to the catch of the day, was a prized Seattle landmark.

Seattle had grown up all around the Market, but the Market didn't really change with it. I hadn't been there in years, but it seemed like a great place to spend a day when there was nothing else to do but be alone in one's thoughts and that's one place I didn't particularly want to be, at least today.

I'm not really sure if anyone who actually lives in Seattle buys anything at the Market. I always thought it was for the tourist trade. It was also a great place to people watch. People from all over the world made the Market a must-see when they were in town, so there was always someone or something fun to watch.

I picked up a Curry Hom Bow at Mee Sum, then crossed the street into the main part of the Market. There's a lot of Market to see. I don't really think you can do it all in a day.

I definitely have my favorites there. Always a Hom Bow at Mee Sum, then some broasted chicken livers and gizzards, chased down by a drink or two at Lowell's.

Lowell's is another Seattle institution. It's been there for as long as anyone can remember. It's not a place you set out to go to, but it is a place where you'll almost always end up – at least if you're at the Market.

I opted to take a booth up top instead of a water view. When you're drinking alone, you usually want something to entertain you and the constant parade of people past the window was like standing on the shore of the Pirates of the Caribbean ride at Disneyland, watching the boats of mesmerized tourists pass by.

After the curry and salt of the chicken and Hom Bow, the double bourbon I ordered was delicious and satisfying, relaxing and fortifying me in the same instant.

I looked out the window at the throng of tourists below, cameras in hand, snapping photos of everything and everyone. I was particularly taken with the one gentleman who insisted on touching the produce in the stalls across the way.

I admit that these pristine veggies and fruits are hard to resist. But the merchants don't want you to touch them as they are not really for sale. There's plenty behind the counter, and that's what they give you. You never pick anything from the front; they don't want you to have it because it's for display only, carefully washed, waxed and stacked.

He didn't seem to understand that, as he continued to insist on touching the merchandise. I can only assume that there was a language barrier for the vendor was now highly animated and mouthing things very slowly. I couldn't make out what he was saying – lip reading is not one of my fortes – but he was obviously not getting his message across because his gestures became more grandiose and equally more futile.

I was so consumed by the circus in the arcade that I hadn't noticed I had company.

"Hey, McCabe. Fancy meeting you here. I didn't picture you as the tourist type."

"I didn't think you were the type either, Darla. Perhaps I should ask what brought you here. A long way from *the strip*, aren't you?"

"Good one, McCabe. Funnn-Y! At least you know you have a career to fall back on when the private eye gig stops working for you."

"Comedian?"

"Now you are being hilarious, McCabe. Comedian? I was thinking more like bouncer at the Lazy Susan," she said, looking out on the continuing saga of miscommunication at the stall across the way. "I can always get you a job there."

"I have one, thanks, Darla. Seriously, what brings you here?"

Darla continued to keep her gaze on the passing parade.

"My work bud Natasha wanted to pick up some arugula for the dinner she's making for her boyfriend," she said. "I told her that it might be fun to tag along. Nothing else to do today."

"Where's Natasha now?"

"Oh, she ditched me. She caught up with me just

down the way and said her boyfriend was picking her up in a bit. That's when I spotted you in here. What a crazy coincidence."

"Yes, it certainly is, Darla. I would have liked to have met your friend."

"Maybe next time, McCabe. Maybe next time."

I asked Darla if she wanted anything. She ordered a screwdriver, a double.

"I used to be a screwdriver guy," I said.

"I know."

"And how would you know that?" I replied with more than a wary eye.

"Silly. All guys go through a screwdriver phase. When they are old enough to drink, they start out with the sweet stuff, things like piña coladas and Smith & Kerns. Once their date makes fun of them, they switch to something a bit more manly."

"Such as?"

"Well, screwdrivers if they are a vodka man. Rum and Coke if they like rum. Something that is still a bit sweet, but has a bit more legs to it. Few guys can make the leap from a piña colada to double bourbon straight up.

"You seem to know an awful lot about what men like, Darla."

"Occupational hazard, McCabe. What else is there to do on stage? It doesn't take a lot of brain power to wiggle your ass, shake your breasts and make men drool so they part with their hard earned dough.

"So, you have a lot of time on your hands," she continued. "You start paying attention to the people in the audience. And men have definite preferences for all sorts of things. All you have to do is learn to be a good student."

"I have a feeling that you're just a fountain of knowledge about all sorts of things men like," I shot back.

"I thought you'd already noticed that, Brewster darling. I gave you a nice sampler back at the house."

"Sampler? I think it was more like rape."

"Give me a break, McCabe. You loved every minute of it. Your pants were off, remember? Your dick was standing at attention, ready to salute anything I was ready to pass by you."

"You know that it was a complete misunderstanding. All that talk about thighs, legs and breasts. How could I have ever imagined that you were talking about the colonel's freaking chicken?"

"That's what I wanted you to think, McCabe. Come on, I know you love a good play on words. Haven't you read through the last 190 pages? I was just giving you what you so desperately wanted: a little mental foreplay."

"Well, it worked. I have to admit, all the double entendre was a bit of a turn on."

"You are so easy, McCabe. A couple turns of a phrase and you're totally turned on. Imagine what you'd do with an entire paragraph. You'd cream your jeans right there and then. An entire page and you'd be cumming for a week."

I had no idea what Darla's hold on me could be. She was hardly my type. Yes, she was a woman. She was breathing. But she was dark haired, a bit on the hefty side, and obviously ridden hard and put away wet more than a time or two.

There was something about her. Maybe it was her intellect. I really do enjoy the dodge and parry of a good verbal duel. It's like sex with your clothes on. She had a way of seeing through me and that was both alluring and alarming.

I was tempted to throw caution to the wind and see if we could go a couple pages, um, rounds. But I hated to mix business with pleasure and as much as a pleasure Darla could potentially be, I needed to keep the two separate, at least until I solved the case.

I pulled out of the gutter and back onto the high road again.

"So, have you seen Darryl lately or heard from him?" I said, returning to the task at hand. "I'd really like to speak with him."

"Do you still think he knows something about these murders? I mean, how would Darryl know Melissa? I can get Lola on a very shaky stretch, but Melissa? I just don't get it."

"I'm not saying he did the deed," I replied, looking deep into her delicious pools that doubled as eyes. "I just wanted to see if he knew anything at all about either of them."

Darla turned to look out the window once more. "No, I haven't heard or seen him. And I have no idea where he is. I am not my brother's keeper, McCabe."

I wondered if she was telling the truth.

"I'd hate to have this come between us," I said.

"Something come between us?" she said, grinning. "You mean this?"

She reached between my legs, grabbing my attention instantly.

"He doesn't seem very excited to see me right now." She squeezed harder. "Does he have a nickname?"

"Oh My god!" I blurted out in agony.

"Interesting name, McCabe. Never heard that one before."

She released her grip and started to laugh. I couldn't help but let out a laugh too, albeit a slightly pained one.

"Well Darla," I said, getting up very slowly from the table. "It was a pleasure seeing you again. I think."

"Brewster, don't go," she said, grasping my hand lightly. "I don't want to be alone today."

"I think it would be a good idea if we part ways now. Plus, I think I need to see my doctor."

I turned to leave, making sure that I didn't look back. I didn't really need to see my doctor. In fact, the whole exchange under the table was kind of titillating.

But I really didn't need to cloud up my mind with a little slip between the sheets right now. Besides, every woman I seemed to come into contact with lately was now laid out on a stainless steel slab in the morgue. Who'd be next?

Mom.

Maybe I should go see good old mom.

Nah, there'd be plenty of time to visit mom later. I really was having quite a nice day and didn't want to ruin it stopping by at mom's. If I just dropped in I'd have to endure the usual crap about meeting my future ex-wife, then I'd have to tell her that my future ex-wives were dying at an alarming pace, and before you know it, I'd get the usual lecture about how I was wasting my life, and how no one wanted to marry a used up middle-aged man in his 30s, especially a dick like me.

And who knows, maybe the killer was stalking me and my mom would be next on the list. On second thought, maybe I should stop by.

Before heading home, I stopped by the office once more to see if Finchley had gotten the report early but there was nothing on my desk. I had a brief glimmer of hope when I saw the answering machine flashing, but the message turned out to be from a bill collector wanting to speak with a Mr. McCabe. I guess he wanted my father. I'm definitely not a mister type of guy.

The next morning came all too early. That blinding orb in the sky was beginning to piss me off, but there was no ready solution, given that my bedroom faced the east and there were no drapes.

Well, there used to be drapes, but they had accidentally caught fire a year or so ago, forcing me to throw them through the open window as a candle tipped over in the midst of an attempted tryst.

That must have been quite the show for the neighbors. The smoke alarm blaring in my apartment, flaming remnants raining down from the bedroom window, all while a very panicked and mostly naked woman fled out my front door, screaming all the way to her car, trying desperately to find her keys while keeping the last shreds of her decency intact, armed only with a French cut bra, a thong and thankfully, a very large purse.

I didn't curse the shiny orb too long on this particular morning because Mother Nature was knocking on my back door with an exit strategy that could not be ignored.

I rolled as quickly as I could out of my bed, mad at myself that I hadn't bothered to get a frame, as rolling to the ground was a dangerous maneuver to attempt when Linda Blair was trying to make a sequel in your backside.

I made it to the bathroom with not a moment to spare. As I let the demons loose, I wondered if it was the pizza seeking its revenge. I guess I shouldn't have retrieved a piece from the pizza's final resting place on top of my soiled shirt. I felt as if I had been poisoned, like I was about to die.

"Poisoned!" I let loose in more ways than one.

What if Melissa's pizza had been purposely poisoned? She would have downed a slice or two and the poison would have had all the time it wanted to shut her system down, dropping her in her tracks. She might not have even been aware that she had been poisoned or that someone wanted to kill her.

The coroner's report would be the arbiter on that.

I decided it was time to take my search for Darryl in a different direction. Darla was of little help, and quite frankly, all that give and take was beginning to get a little confusing.

I couldn't help but wonder if she was covering up for her brother. But why? They didn't seem to be that close. At least that's what she said, anyway. I wanted to believe her but somewhere in that private eye mind of mine there was a niggling shadow of doubt.

It was lucky for me that Nurse Cratchett wasn't Finchley's only love interest. It seems that a friend of his down at Motor Vehicles didn't know about the nurse and was still seeing him as well.

I had no idea he was such a lady's man. I seemed to have a knack for dead end relationships and now dead ones, too. And he's out taking numbers and remembering their names. Darla was the only one who had taken a shine to me in a while, except for that flameout in my apartment and the resulting 50-yard dash in the buff.

Fortunately, Darla's mother was not only alive, but still driving. Finch was able to pick up the address of one Mabel Diamond.

I hopped in the Monster and sped off to the address, just off Highway 167 in an area known as East Hill. I give the founders of Kent credit for at least understanding how a compass worked and adding direction to the destination. But why anyone lived there was still beyond me. It's not a place you want to be from, let alone still call home.

The house wasn't hard to find. A quaint rambler in the older part of the neighborhood. What am I saying? It's not like there had been any development on the East Hill in years, except for hundreds of faceless apartments built for Lord knows whom. I mean, who makes it their life's goal to live in Kent?

But no matter. I was only here on a quick visit. I was hoping that Mabel was home. I don't usually call ahead, knowing that someone could just as easily skip out on me as be home if they knew I was on my way. The element of surprise can definitely work in one's favor.

The doorbell rang like someone was home. I heard the chirpy bark of a small dog getting louder as it ran to the door, pointlessly trying to ward off intruders.

In between barks I could hear a step-step-drag, step-step-drag sound; most unnerving. I wondered if Darla's mom had a clubfoot or something.

She didn't. Instead, Mabel had a walker, complete with the requisite tennis balls that her poor dog still tried to tussle with, his feeble mind never comprehending that she was trying to get around her house, not play some kind of sick game of fetch.

From behind the barred screen door she told me off to within an inch of my life.

"What do you want, you slicker?" she said. "Are you trying to sell me something? Do you know how many of your kind I have buried in the backyard? I'm running out of room."

She was a thin, spindly woman, wracked by the passage of time, her better days behind her, her twilight years ahead, until that unavoidable day when the fates turn her light to the off position for the final time and the power bill that was her life goes unpaid.

"Mrs. Diamond, I'm Brewster McCabe, a friend of

your daughter Darla and a private eye. I'm trying to find Darryl, your son."

"He's no son of mine. Not these days, at least. Prick! Well, come in, I need some tea and you'll do just fine making me some."

I followed her ever so slowly down the hall to the kitchen in the back. It was readily apparent that she had already been thinking about the tea, given that the kettle was heating on the stove and a teacup was on the counter.

"Well, get to it, young man. I ain't got all day," she said. "I could keel over at any minute, you know!"

I could see where Darla acquired her womanly charms. Apples and trees.

I boiled the water and steeped the tea, bringing two cups into the living room.

"Are you out of your mind, man? Did I say you could have a cup of tea? Did I invite you? I'm living on a fixed income, you shit! I can't feed the entire world."

It looks like she had already tried to do just that with Darryl.

"Sorry, Mrs. Diamond. I just really wanted to have a great cup of tea."

She sighed. "Suit yourself then. It would take too long to dry those tea leaves out again anyway. Just leave a quarter on the counter as you leave and we'll call it square then."

I began to thank her, when it occurred to me that she had forgotten why I was here.

"Well, nice to see you, son," she said. "Don't let the

door hit you on your way out."

"But I wanted to talk to you about Darryl, remember?"

"Darryl's not here, you piece of crap. Ran off with that shithole and I haven't heard from him since. I just can't get my head around this whole homosexual thing he says he is. When he said he was gay all those years I just thought he was happy."

"What shithole?" I asked.

"Blimpie."

"Blimpie?" I replied. "Is that his name?"

"No, it's a sandwich chain, you dolt. And you say you're a private eye. You don't know shit, do you?"

I knew of the sandwich chain, of course. But I just played into the hand I was dealt.

"So, tell me what happened."

"What is this, *This Is Your Life*? Why should I tell you anything, shithead?"

I must admit, I really wanted to smack the old broad. She reminded me too much of my own mom. Instead, I handed her my last twenty, hoping that it would open her up. It did.

"So my son is at Blimpies one day. He runs into this guy who'd been eating there. Ate there every damned day it turns out, and dropped something like 200 pounds. So Darryl and he start talking and they hit it off. Damned if I know why. They end up meeting every day at the store down the road, makin' horny eyes at one another, blah, blah, freakin' blah!"

"Before I know it, dipweed Darryl thinks he's in love with this guy. Love! Can you believe it? Like he knows jackshit about love!

"I won't have anything to do with the guy, mind you."

"Blimpie?"

"No, shit Sherlock! You know, you should be a detective, asshole! Real quick on the uptake."

"So have you seen Darryl since?" I said, trying hard not to belt her.

"Only a couple of times. He goes south of the border plenty where Blimpie's concerned, if you get my drift," she said, winking. "But he doesn't cross the border to see the woman who gave him life. Bastard!"

A couple photos on the mantle caught my eye.

"So, he's up in Canada then?" I said, getting up to have a closer look.

"Yeah, they're shacking up in Vancouver, living, loving and enjoying the Big Salami."

"We don't need to go there," I replied.

"The sandwich dipweed. Get your mind outta the freakin' gutter. We're talking about my son, remember?"

As we spoke, I gave the photos a good once over.

A framed shot of Darla and Darryl at the all-you-can-eat pie contest at the state fair, fighting over the gold medal they had tied for. Santa sitting on the kid's knees for Christmas, looking very relieved it wasn't the other way around. Darla and Darryl dressed as Violet

Beauregarde and Augustus Gloop for Halloween, their mother hovering over them with a big bar of chocolate as a very believable Willy Wonka. And a picture of the two kids playing dress up, each portraying the other so well you could barely tell them apart.

"Nice family photos," I said. "I…"

"You can leave now," she said, rising from the sofa with some help from the walker.

"But…"

"L-E-A-V-E! Is it that you can't spell or you can't comprehend, prick?"

"One more question, then I'll go," I finally said, more than a little perturbed.

"If that's what it takes to get you out of here, shoot!"

I wanted to take that as an invitation. I wouldn't have thought twice about plugging her right between the eyes, just so I could hear the bullet ricochet through her skull like a game of pinball. But then Darla would be consumed with grief and give me even more grief about icing her mother.

"If you got a question, spit it out or get out," she said impatiently.

"What did you do for a living?"

"Customer Service, ass-wipe. Now get the hell out of my house. And stay away from my family while you're at it!"

I never knew that an elderly woman, anchored to a walker, could move so quickly or spryly. As I made my way to the door she managed to spank me a time or two with the walker. As I had my sights set on making a quick exit out the door, I was unable to turn around, even ever so briefly, to see how she was managing to do it.

The door slammed behind me and I stood there in the crisp sunshine, contemplating the ever-dueling concepts of nurture vs. nature. If I were ever on Jeopardy I'd have to go with, "What is nurture for a thousand, Alex?"

My own family was mostly nature with a jigger of nurture thrown in for good measure. As you might recall, three brothers, one no longer with us, the other two not having spoken to me since the day my wife found my hand in someone else's cookie jar.

In a way, I really admired Mabel. My own little girl rarely had contact with me, except on birthdays divisible by three and even then it would just be a card with a half-hearted scribble of a name that I think is hers. Oh, the money Hallmark could make with pre-signed cards. A simple scribble that you'd readily convince yourself is your son's or daughter's, and that they really took the time to pick out a card that meant something to them, rather than grab the first one off the rack, look at the price on the back and buy the cheapest one they could find in the shortest amount of time.

At least Mabel had all those good memories. I just had the check stubs of seemingly endless child support payments and a stack of yellowing Instamatic 110 photos, waiting for the day that will probably never come when I finally have the time or desire to paste them into a photo album.

I'm not sure what Kent does to a guy, but it certainly made me question my life on the way back to the office.

If Suicide Hotline had their headquarters in Kent, their own employees would be their most frequent callers. But they'd call only once before realizing that nothing on the other side could be as horrible as living in Kent.

I stopped at a corner drug to check my messages. Sure enough, there was one from Finchley. He had the coroner's report. I called him back and he told me he could meet me back at the office in an hour. We could go over the report together then.

I decided to kill a little time in the drugstore. I thought I might be able to pick the druggist's brain a bit about prescriptions that could be poisonous in the right doses. I couldn't get that idea out of my mind, that perhaps there was a drug out there that was barely traceable or even totally untraceable that could debilitate someone, or outright kill them.

It was a slow day for drugs, obviously. There was no one in the A&H, which was fine with me. I figured the druggist might have a little time to shoot the breeze.

Before sucking his brain dry of information, I picked a random item off of the shelf and used it as my excuse to speak with him.

"Can you tell me the best way to use these?" I asked, trying to look nonchalant.

"Well, first you'd want to get a sex change, unless you have a misses or a teenage daughter. They're sanitary napkins, sir!"

Damn! I really need to pay more attention before I try to act nonchalant.

"Um, yes, um, it's for the misses. She hasn't used this

particular brand before. I thought I would save her the trouble of calling you."

He knew I was full of it.

He looked me in the eye, smiled, turned his head tellingly, and then we both laughed. He had figured I wasn't the kind of guy who would ever pick up a box of sanitary napkins willingly – or unwillingly.

"Ya got me, uh, Sam!" I said, looking at the nametag on his lab coat. "Got me dead to right!"

"So, let me guess, Mister, Mister…"

"McCabe. Brewster McCabe."

I handed him my card.

"A private eye, eh?" he said. "Thought so. The fedora was a dead giveaway. And what brings you into my neck of the woods today, Detective McCabe?"

It was refreshing to be called detective for a change. In my line of work I am often called many things, but detective? By the thugs, lugs, whores, jingoes and dolts I had to deal with on a daily basis? I was lucky to be called Brewster or McCabe.

"Well, sir," I said. "I'm curious about drugs that could paralyze an individual. Not kill them outright necessarily, but maybe cause their heart and lungs to eventually fail, to the point that any autopsy would say they were asphyxiated."

"Hmm," he said, stroking the goatee on his chin. "Nothing that's mainline prescription. Let me go in the back and search some of my reference works. It would have to be something unusual not to show up in today's blood, urine and toxicology test results. Got me stumped on that one."

Sam excused himself for a moment while I returned the napkins to their rightful place on the shelf. As I did, an elderly woman standing next to me glanced over, muttering not so softly, "Perv."

I would have explained the mix up but Sam had re-emerged from the dark, secret catacombs of the pharmacy, looking quite pleased with himself.

"Coniine," he said, almost gleefully. "It's the oily liquid that comes from hemlock. Used in lots of the Classics, you know, to kill someone off without leaving a trace."

"Coniine? Never heard of it."

"Hamlet?"

"Is that the manufacturer?" I asked.

Sam rolled his eyes. "You don't do much reading, do you McCabe? Hamlet. Shakespeare. The Classics."

"I confess, I've never had time to read any Shakespeare. Not a big fan of the mystery genre."

Sam looked like he was going to die right then and there of laughter. It took him a few moments to collect himself before he was able to continue.

"Well, they would refer to it as hemlock back in Shakespeare's day. But coniine would do the trick if someone were trying to cover his or her tracks."

"How does it work?" I asked.

He pulled his reference book up from his side and plopped it on the counter. He quickly went to the page he had marked with a Post-It.

His finger crossed the page as he read:

"Symptoms will begin to occur within 30 minutes. Death will not be instantaneous, but may take several hours, depending on the dose. The person may remain conscious and aware until breathing stops due to respiratory paralysis. Lower limbs are affected first, rendering the person unable to move. Eventually there will be a convulsion but it may be disguised by the paralysis and simply manifest itself as a shudder."

"Where would you get coniine?"

"Nowhere around here, by any stretch," Sam said, looking back down at his book of mystical spells and incantations, as that's how old the book looked to be.

"It would have to come from the Mediterranean, I would imagine, if it were in finished form. Hemlock as a species is pretty common, even in the U.S., but you can't make coniine just by tapping a tree and sucking the sap out of it. It's not exactly maple syrup. You'd have to know the tricks of the trade to do it right, especially if you only wanted to incapacitate a person and not kill them outright."

"Thanks," I said. "I appreciate the information, Sam."

"Not sure how much use it is to you, but you're welcome," he said. "Not planning to kill anyone with it, are you detective?"

"Hamlet," I said, turning to leave. Whoever he is.

Chapter 16

I met Finchley back at the office. True to form he had the coroner's report on Melissa. He was sitting at my desk, thumbing through it when I entered.

"Uh, hey boss!" he said, jumping to his feet, looking somewhat embarrassed.

"Hey, Finchley. Go ahead and sit down. I don't mind."

He looked a bit confused since I would regularly shoo him away from my desk.

I took the seat across from the desk. "Just give me the Reader's Digest version."

"Same thing as Lola, from what I can tell, McCabe. Just a few marks, no sign of a struggle. Toxicology came back fairly normal. Just some mild tranquilizers in her system, prescribed. Otherwise, apparent cause of death was asphyxiation. It's like they made a carbon copy of the last report."

I was hardly surprised. By now it was becoming clear that these two murders were no coincidence. They were cold, calculated and connected.

But how? I still couldn't figure out what the connection was between the two girls.

At first, I thought it may have been Bubba. Perhaps Melissa was mixed up in some blackmail scam Bubba was running or was doing illegal drugs. But that just didn't make any sense, especially since toxicology didn't show any trace of drugs, except those that were prescribed and even those were pretty soft core.

Darryl could be the connection. But I couldn't imagine that Lola had come into contact with Darryl since their Associated Grocers days. And Melissa was hardly the type to move in the same circles as Darryl, or Lola for that matter. And she's wasn't the type to be caught dead at Dirk's.

Dead at Dirk's. I couldn't help but think about the irony of that. We always joked about taking matters into our own hands when we dined at Dirk's, inviting the Reaper to finally drop by whenever we ate there. Instead the Reaper visited Lola and Melissa, picking up their tab instead.

"What about you, McCabe?"

"I'm fine, thanks, Finchley," I said, sitting back in the chair. "Just one of those days."

"No boss, I mean what about you? What if you're the lynchpin here? What if you're the connection? What if someone was trying to get to you for some reason?"

It was a clarion of clarity for Finchley. A moment in time when he was clear as a bell and I was as cloudy as a Seattle day.

"Geez, Finch! You may just be on to something there. But why? Why me?"

"Maybe someone has a score to settle with you, McCabe," Finchley replied. "You've pissed off a lot of people over the years, I'm sure. Any private eye worth his salt would. Maybe someone just wants to even the score. Hurt you like you hurt them."

I always thought Finchley would make a great detective again one day. And today, if ever so briefly, was the day.

"Finch, I have to say, I think you're ready to go out on your own again. Consider yourself reloaded into that shotgun known as life, my friend."

"Thanks boss," he said, closing the folder on the desk and rising from the chair. "I think I'm good right where I'm at right now. You need me as much as I need you. We make a great team."

"That we do, Finchley," I admitted. "That we do. But don't think for a moment that you're going to get a raise just because you're kissing up to me like this."

"I don't know McCabe. It's a good time to give me a raise since you're not paying me anything anyway."

I let go a laugh, a laugh that really needed to happen. The days since Lola's murder had been indeed dark ones and even a brief moment of levity and laughter seemed to lift a tremendous weight off of me.

"Well, I'll double your salary then, Finchley," I said. "Now let's figure out who could possibly want to get back at me. Why don't you pull out the case files from the cabinet and I'll go through my phone logs and see if there could be something there."

We spent most of the afternoon and evening going through every file and phone call. Nothing. At least nothing that was glaringly obvious. Sure, I had pissed off some people. What private eye hasn't? But most of my clients were either two-bitters who weren't bitter or jailbirds doing time in jail. I had never made it to the big time, dealing with people who could afford to put a contract out on me. I mean, a Benjamin, even twins, couldn't get you a meeting with a hit man who'd be able to hit the broad side of a barn, let alone dispatch someone in a way that couldn't be traced. That took some big bucks.

Damn, another apparent dead end, even though Finchley's hunch still seemed to have some legs. I was the only thread that connected the two women and the two murders. Darryl was a close second, but the exact connection, if there was one, was still unknown.

I decided that it was time to go for a walk. Even though Pioneer Square was the resident domain of bums, whores, druggies and other fringes of society, I thought of it as my second home. I knew every nook and cranny of the place, from where to get a drink before hours to where to go after hours for some filling food and a bartender's ear to bend.

I strolled past the Klondike Museum on Main, heading past Occidental Park. I heard a fire engine pull out from the firehouse around the corner, the siren bouncing between the buildings, creating an eerie sound as it cut its way through the still air like a dull knife.

I crossed the street as the engine passed and ducked into Waterfall Park. It seemed a bit strange that such a wonderful urban oasis could exist in one of the less favored parts of town. I've always enjoyed this little hideaway, the two-story waterfall offering a slight moment of Zen in a bustling city, allowing me to clear my mind and let the nonsense of everyday life – the overdue bills, the lack of a life and unresolved relationship issues – slip aside, if for one brief moment.

The sound of the falls was hypnotic, lulling me into a trance of momentary peace and quiet. It was like being transported to another place and another time.

I must've drifted off for a bit, for I was awakened by the soft touch of a hand on my shoulder.

"Finchley, really? Here? Now?"

"I didn't know we were into kinky nicknames, already," came the reply. "Darla will do for now."

It was hardly a voice I expected to hear.

"What are you doing here?" I said, more than a little bit surprised.

"I'm stalking you McCabe. I follow you everywhere, didn't you know?" She let go a laugh, one so loud it drowned out the waterfall for a moment.

"Seriously, I stopped by your office to speak with you and the guy there said you went out for a walk. I always loved this spot and took a chance that you did too. Beats walking around and around town trying to find you. If you weren't here, then hey, I get to enjoy the tranquility of the waterfall for a bit before heading home."

She got up for a moment, walked over to the waterfall and reached into her pocket for something. In one motion she turned, closed her eyes tight, and flung the coin into the fountain, as if making a wish.

"God, I hope it comes true, Brewster," she said, before suddenly changing the subject. "Did you know that this place is on the site of the original UPS office? It was founded in Seattle, ya know. Their first office was right under the sidewalk, right here."

"And then the sons of bitches moved to Atlanta," I said.

"Turncoats," we said at the same time.

It was the right time at the right moment. Without even thinking, I kissed her long and hard. My toes tingled as our souls truly met for the first time.

She lingered for a while, then stepped back a bit.

"Wow! That was unexpected," she said, turning back to the fountain.

I came up behind her and reached my arms around her waist. She didn't fight me, but she didn't encourage me either.

"McCabe, I think it's time. I'll tell you what. Meet me at my house at 7 tonight and we'll take this whole thing to another level. Have a little dinner and if you don't behave yourself, maybe you'll get some delicious dessert – me. I am going to blow your mind, McCabe."

Chapter 17

I was torn about whether to make my date. Professionally, it was a little unethical, but hey, I'm a private eye not a priest. It's not like it was the first unethical thing I've done and it's not like the Private Eye Association was going to put me on probation or kick me out. I wasn't a member.

Before arriving at Darla's I drove around the block several times. Not because I was early, but because once again I was lost in the maze of streets they call Somerset. I had just about given up when I saw the characteristically out of place blue house on the block of beige colored houses, the hallmark of a homeowner's association out of control and hell high on power.

Obviously Darla didn't kowtow to the mainstream and maybe that's why I liked her so. I thought to ask her if she ever thought of putting a 15' pole in the front lawn and never fly a flag from it, seeing how long it took the association president to figure out it was a stripper pole, not a flagpole.

I parked the Monster out on the street and went up the walk to the door. I rang the doorbell, dot on 7 p.m.

The door opened, but it wasn't Darla doing the greeting.

"Um, Darryl?" I said, a bit surprised.

"That's right!" he said, shaking my hand. "And you

must be here to see Darla though I have to say, I'd rather it was me."

"Well, this is your lucky day, Darryl. I would love to spend a few minutes with you if you have the time."

I could swear that he was licking his lips at the thought. I could almost imagine him making those unsettling calls to Lola.

Maybe my private eye instincts weren't so far out of whack after all. He was a few board feet short of a patio, but this was my first chance to look him in the eye.

"That'd be fine with me," he said. "Darla's running a little late anyway and she wanted to shower and primp before you arrived. Let's go into the living room, shall we?"

I took a seat on the sofa; Darryl sat across me on the loveseat, which looked more like an overstuffed chair, at least with him in it.

"So, Darryl, Darla tells me that you're living in Canada now, eh?"

"That's right, eh. Found a great life up there in North Washington, as me and my bestie like to call it."

"Has Darla mentioned much about what I do or what I've been working on?"

"Only that you're some kind of private investigator. A bit of a dick, eh?" he chortled and snorted. "Oh, and you think I'm somehow connected to a murder or two down here, which is pretty damned funny."

"Funny? Two people are dead and you think it's funny?"

"Not funny dead, eh," he replied. "Funny that I'm a possible suspect."

"Do you remember Lola Chase? She worked with you at AG."

"Of course, I remember, Lola," he replied. "Who wouldn't? I may be a gay guy but I still appreciate a lovely woman – maybe it's jealousy."

He gave me a wry wink.

"She's dead, you know."

Darryl stopped smiling and looked down at the ground, then, somberly, he looked back at me. "Such a nice girl. She was a great friend to me at a time when I had few friends in this world."

"Where were you on the 10th, Darryl?"

"I was up in Canada, working with my friend on a commercial for Blimpies, you know, the sandwich chain. You can call him and verify that I was with him all day, eh. I'll get you his number if you'd like. You can also check with the director."

If his story checked out , it would be another dead end. I filled him in on a few of the details, how Lola was being tormented by a stalker who made unsettling calls at all hours, never speaking, only breathing heavily and smacking his lips, as if he had walked the counterbalance to the top of Queen Anne so he could indulge in the Royal Fork buffet there.

There was no unusual reaction to any of it. He just stared blankly, looking repulsed a bit any time the story got gorier.

"I also think the same guy had something to do with

the death of Melissa Owens."

"I heard about that up north. It was in the Vancouver papers. Rich girl I hear. You knew her, eh?"

"I knew them both. That's what brings me into the case," I said. "It's personal. The police are doing their investigation, but I wanted my own answers. I'm sure that you've also popped up on their radar by now, but if your witnesses can corroborate your alibi, you shouldn't have any trouble passing the polygraph once Detective Grist gets your scent."

"Then there's no need to change my plans for tonight," he replied, jotting a few numbers down on a piece of paper. "Here's the phone numbers of the director and my friend. Feel free to use the phone here. I would hate to be late for my dinner date with a couple of serious drag queens up on Capital Hill."

I called the first number, a production company. Their service answered and I asked for the director. A minute or two went by before I was connected. He confirmed what Darryl had said, saying they were on the set from noon until 3 a.m. the next morning. Darryl was with his partner the entire time.

"Well, Darryl, looks like you're off the hook," I said, sitting back down on the sofa. "No need to check with your friend. The director cleared you, saying you were on the set, just as you said. A quick check with Customs will confirm that you didn't somehow sneak across the border at the crack of early."

"Great, then we're good to go, eh?" he said, getting up to leave. "I'll leave you to wait for Darla if you don't mind. I need to scoot out of here in a few minutes if I'm going to get to the church on time."

"I have one more question, then you can keep your date," I interjected.

"Shoot," he said. "But be quick about it."

"Do you have a pair of tennis shoes?"

"Do I look like the running type, McCabe?" he replied, looking a bit confused. "But to answer your somewhat silly question, sure I do. Who doesn't? It's the Northwest. Everyone has at least one pair of tenny runners in their closet. But look at me. Do I look like I would ever make that kind of fashion statement? At least in public?"

"I can see your point, Darryl. Just a routine question."

"Routine? Maybe if you're a track coach."

Darryl headed down the hall. He must've stopped to talk to Darla for a moment as I heard the muffled strains of conversation briefly. Too bad I couldn't hear what they were saying, but it sounded pleasant enough. With a slam of the back screen door, Darryl departed.

Women. Even if they say seven you'll wait at least until 7:30, often longer. They never seem to be in a rush. Not that I am such an expert, but I've been left waiting many times in my life. Often for days at a time, as my date would sometimes be a no show, me assuming that she simply forgot or got tied up somewhere.

Tied up somewhere. Geez, I crack myself up sometimes.

I decided to pass the time by helping myself to a

drink, sure that Darla wouldn't mind if I poured me one or two to pass the time.

Her liquor cabinet looked like the top shelf of a Washington State Liquor store. There was everything imaginable. Like a kid in a candy store I rummaged through the stock, finding a bottle of Maker's Mark that was begging to be opened. I twisted the lid and the faint yet delicious scent of smooth bourbon rose to greet my welcoming nostrils.

I grabbed a chimney and poured me a tall one.

The Chairman of the Board was now crooning down the hall, setting a mood filled with intrigue. She's got great taste in music, I thought. Who doesn't like Sinatra?

I returned to the sofa and kicked back. It was then that I spotted a copy of *Stripper's Monthly* on the coffee table.

I became consumed by the article on pole-vaulting, which it turned out, had nothing to do with the Summer Olympics. Wow, I never knew that anyone could do that with a pole.

It was so engaging that I didn't even notice Darla entering the room.

"Something catch your eye, McCabe? And here I was hoping it was me."

I looked up to see Darla. She was dressed to kill. It was as if she had read my mind and found every piece of Kryptonite that made me weak for a woman, from the fetching see-through lace top to the stiletto heels on her boots.

"You mean that article isn't as interesting now?" She

spun in place. "Like what you see?"

I liked what I saw all right. I got up to greet her and gave her a hugging long, um, a longing hug... a long hug.

"The groping comes later, McCabe. First we'll have dinner. I'm famished."

She took me by the hand and led me into the dining room.

"Sit down baby while I see what's cooking, besides us that is."

Whatever it was it smelled divine.

"So," she said, "You finally got to meet Darryl. Feel better about it all now? I told you Darryl wasn't the killing kind."

"I don't know if I feel better, Darla. I'm back at square one with two stiffs and no suspects."

"I can make that three stiffs, but you'll have to wait until after dinner," she said, stirring pots in more ways than one.

She returned to the room, armed with a large glass of red wine.

"Sorry, McCabe, bad joke. I didn't mean to make light of this. I knew they were your friends, if not more."

"Let's not go there tonight, Darla. I just want to enjoy a fairly normal night for a change. I need to get off the crazy rollercoaster I've been on and take a slow turn on the carousel."

"That could be fun," she said, a twinkle in her eye. "Never done it on a carousel. I'm more of a Scrambler girl."

"I'm more of a Zipper man, myself," I shot back. "Love them."

"Like the one that goes all the way down the back of my top, Brew?"

"Yes, I couldn't help but notice."

"Well, you'll have to fantasize about where it leads to a little longer. I really am starving."

She returned to the kitchen. I could hear plates rattling and silverware being stacked. The senses were overloading with desire for a really good meal, one that didn't come from a rock-hard box pulled out of the freezer or a short order cook. If it tasted half as good as it smelled, I was going to be one happy camper.

"Need any help in there?" I said, as the minutes passed.

"Not at all, I have everything handled. Just finishing up the sauce and I'll be in in a jiff."

"I must say, Darla, I'm really enjoying the delightful tennis match we're having so far."

"You mean the mental foreplay?" she said. "I hope you brought a couple extra balls to the volley tonight. You're gonna need them."

Point. Match. All that was left was for me to jump over the fishnets and congratulate the winner. The game was over before it began.

"Don't think I'm that easy, McCabe," she said, carrying in two mounds of food that I was sure had to be on plates somewhere underneath. "I can be had, but you'll have to work for it."

Darla definitely knew her way around the kitchen.

"I hope you like Greek," she said. "I made these from old family recipes."

As I dug into the pile I could tell she had put a lot of work into dinner. Leg of Lamb with Potatoes, Spanakopita and a little Greek Salad, some of my favorites.

I must admit that the company, food and top shelf booze was a nice respite from the weeks of sleepless nights, heartburn, dead ends and run-ins with Grist.

"So this is what normal people do with their evenings," I said, biting down on a second leg of lamb, relishing its perfection.

"Isn't this what everyone wants, McCabe? A reason to go home instead of drowning their sorrows night after night at a raunchy strip club or seedy bar?"

"We're hardly normal, Darla. I'm a private eye and you're a… a…"

"You can say it, McCabe," she said, taking another sip of wine. "A stripper. Or if you want it to be a little more tasteful in mixed company, how about an exotic dancer then? I'm good with it. I make a pretty good living and I feel pretty damned powerful doing it."

I was intrigued. "How is that?"

"Look, I make men have their little wet dreams. They can fantasize about me all they want as they go about their day, working for the man, taking that one last meeting before they head home to their dreary little house frau, wondering when they'll get that promotion that will never come, all the time wishing they could be free to be who they are and not have to suck up to the boss day in and day out.

"Me? I give them that freedom. I give them the fantasy. That little woman in the 'burbs gets laid because her husband is thinking of me up on that stage, that he's doing me instead. His workday is just a little more palpable because he can sit at his desk and think of me wrapped around that pole, pretending that I'm climbing him instead. And at the end of the day, it's me he comes to see over and over again because unlike the dreary wife back home and the dead end job, I deliver the goods. I make him feel like he's the man, that I am looking at him when I dance, that he could have me anytime he wants."

"Can he?" I said.

"Oh, come on, McCabe," she replied. "We know how this works. I've already decided if you're going to get lucky tonight. You're still sitting there wondering. I have all the power. All women do."

"Well?"

"Well what?" she said smiling. "Let's dance some, then we'll see."

I freshened both of our drinks as the strains of Strangers in the Night echoed from the hi-fi. Darla had dimmed the lights and I could see her silhouette as she sashayed in front of the large picture window that looked out on the neighbor's house across the street.

"I love to drive them crazy," she said, swaying to the music. "The husband over there is just like all the others. Judging me, but all the time wondering what it would be like to be with me."

I took Darla by the hand and spun her slowly, putting my right hand around her waist. She seemed surprised that I knew how to dance.

"Well, McCabe. You're light on those private eye loafers of yours. Where did you learn to dance like that?"

"Just one of the many things I've picked up along the way," I said, moving her effortlessly around the floor. "I was following a dance school owner once who was trying to do the mambo with a dame who wasn't his wife. I took some lessons while I got the lay of the land, figuring out the best way to catch him in the act."

"Did you?"

"Did I?!" I said. "Caught them in the checkroom, checking each other out on her fur. The pictures were beautifully lit, I must say, and his wife ended up with a hefty alimony check and the dance studio."

"And you got lessons," she said.

Strangers in the Night came to an end and we kissed, long and hard. She took my hand and led me down the hall as Frank continued to sing to a now empty room.

"Let's continue our all-you-can-eat in the bedroom, she said softly.

"I have a feeling I'm going to be in heaven by the end of the night," I said, not offering a bit of resistance.

"You can count on it, McCabe."

As soon as it had started, it ended. I stowed the

rubber sheets and mayonnaise while Darla relished the moment.

"I hate having crumbs between the sheets," she said, "And believe me, I've had a lot of them."

"Maybe you shouldn't be offering an all you can eat experience in the sack, Darla. You're sure to draw a lot of crumbs, like flies are drawn to honey."

"Honey," she said. "I forgot the damned honey! Dammit! How is anyone supposed to get their fill when there's no damned honey to spread around my delicious, warm muffin."

"The muffin, yes. It's still between your legs I presume?"

She reached down, and like a magician doing the big finale, she pulled the muffin from between the sheets.

"A dame like you is the reason I keep these latex gloves handy," I said, letting it snap her thigh as I took it off. "Just in case things get a little messy. And I have to say Darla, you're a bit of a mess in the sack. A delectable mess, but a mess nonetheless. Any Spanakopita left?"

"Here, sweetie," she said. "It's the last piece you'll have for awhile."

I smiled as she snuggled in next to me. Between the food and the loving, I was spent.

I've always enjoyed a woman's boudoir. There's something so romantic about it, like you're stepping into an inner sanctum that you can only gain entrance to by favor.

I don't really know where women get all these frilly,

foamy, fluffy things. I could spend all day haunting the thrift shops and second hand stores I frequent and no matter what I do, no matter how hard I try, I'll end up with a bunch of manly-man décor that's stiff as a board.

Even her bed was frilly. There must've been five layers of sheets, blankets and comforters on it and enough pillows for a sultan to seat a harem. The sheets were silky smooth, as if they were made from a thousand threads. Above, the soft gauze of the canopy spilled down and over the four posts of dark mahogany, hand carved wood.

I didn't have a boudoir, not even a bedframe. It was a cinch that Darla wouldn't be invited to my man pad any time soon, at least until I could afford to hire a decorator – or move.

By now, Darla had dozed off. I thought briefly about doing that thing a lot of men do and sneak off in the dead of night, leaving the woman to wonder what she had done wrong or if she had just been too easy.

This time leaving was out of the question, largely because my arm was trapped under the nape of Darla's neck and there was no way to wiggle free without gnawing it off.

Instead, I just lay there, waiting for Winkin,' Blinkin' and Nod to do their dirty work, hoping that if they did, that they'd be quick about it, for I was wiped.

Chapter 18

When I awoke, Darla was nowhere in sight. I was alone in her room, so sublimely comfortable that I felt as if I would be unable to move even if I had wanted to.

It wasn't until I wanted to move that I discovered I couldn't. Somewhere in the night I had been tied down, the four posters serving as anchors for the silk ties that had been tied around my wrists and ankles.

This was definitely not good. Well, it could be good, but it could also be very, very bad. I didn't have to wait long for the answer.

Darla walked back in wearing nothing but a smile.

"How are ya doing this morning?" she said. "Did you get a good night's sleep?"

"Yes, delightful. A little surprised that I'm now tied up. I'm pretty sure I wasn't this way when I went to sleep."

"Not to worry," she replied, somewhat coolly. "It's all part of the plan I have for you today."

"Plan?" I asked.

"You didn't think I invited you over for an evening of fierce loving without having a plan."

"Will I be clued into this so called plan at any point?" I asked, tugging at the ties that became tighter with each twist and turn.

"In good time, McCabe, in good time. Now, let's get this little game started, shall we?"

She sat down on the edge of the bed. "Here's how this works. I ask you a question and you give me an answer. And each time you lie to me, I'm going to pull out one of the hairs on your body."

I laughed, albeit a bit nervously. "Cut the crap, Darla," I implored. "I really need to get to work. There's a killer out there somewhere and I'm worried that he's going to strike again."

Darla grabbed the robe hanging from the bedpost and loosely tied it around her. She then settled herself next to me, her head propped up by her arm.

"I'd gag you right now but I need answers and 'Mmmm, mmmm' isn't going to cut it."

"I could just scream," I warned. "Someone is bound to hear me."

"Like they haven't heard screaming come from this bedroom before," she said nonchalantly.

"Now, first question. Did you and Lola ever do one another?"

"What kind of bullshit question is that?" I asked. "It's none of your business really."

"Oops. Wrong answer," she said pulling out one of the hairs on my chest with tweezers she had pulled from the pocket of her robe.

"Ouch! That hurt! Is this some kind of sado-masochism game we're playing?"

"Think of it instead as a game of 'Truth or Hair,' McCabe," she replied, laughing. "And remember, you're the one deciding how painful this is going to be. Now, back to the question at hand and this time think about the consequences before you answer. Did you and Lola ever do the big nasty together?"

"I'm not playing this sick game, Darla. You think this is the first time I've been tortu... OUCH! O.K., O.K., The answer is no, we never did. I never even dated her."

Darla clamped onto another hair, this time, one below the equator.

"Let's up the anty a bit, shall we? It'll make things move along more quickly if you have more skin, or should I say hair, in the game.

"So let's say that what you said is true and that Lola was just a wet dream for you up until now? Did you have hopes that it would go any further?"

"Yes," I replied. "But that will never happen now, obviously."

With a quick pluck another hair was harvested, one from a much more fragile place.

"Hey, I told the truth, didn't I?"

"Yes," she said. "But I didn't like the answer."

I could quickly tell that this was not a game I was going to win. I could only hope that it would be a quick game of Twenty Questions as I really didn't have a lot of hair to spare.

"Can we move on?" I begged.

She plucked another hair. "I ask the questions here. You don't. I can see this isn't going as well as I expected. I think we need to kick things up another notch."

Darla made her way over to the dresser, pulling a tapered candle from her top drawer and a book of matches. She took her time lighting the candle, as if it were some kind of ritual. The smell of sulfur reminded me of the Wicked Witch in the Wizard of Oz. This may have been typecasting.

O.K., so this was a sick game, but it must be some kind of foreplay, as she was lighting candles now. She cupped her hand around the flickering flame as she made her way back to the bed.

"This should help," she said.

Instead of placing the candle on the nightstand, she poured a puddle of it on my chest. The pain was excruciating as the melted wax pooled and then hardened around one of the few clumps of chest hair I owned.

"Now, McCabe," she said. "We were talking about your hard-on for Lola and that you thought you might be able to knock her up before she was knocked off.

"Let's move on, shall we?" she said, wedging the still burning candle into a candlestick on the table next to her.

She rubbed my chest slowly before bringing her fingernails to bear, leaving four red lines from my neck to the now hardened pool of wax.

"You and Melissa were an item, right? Back before she got all that work done. When she was still a bag lady."

"Yes," I replied, tugging at the ties. "So what does this have to do with anything now?"

"Oops, you asked another question. That's gonna really hurt." She found the edge of the wax and tugged on it, then let go of her grip. "Scared ya, didn't I?"

As I began to laugh nervously she ripped the wax off in a single fluid motion that was painful yet something of a rush.

"Goddamn it! Are you mental or something? Can you just let me go?"

"I'll let that one pass, since I can't tell if it's a question or a pitiful plea for mercy," she said, picking up the candle again.

"Who else have you been seeing behind my back, McCabe? I'll give you some time to frame your answer."

"Behind your back?" I said. "Are we in a relationship of some kind? When did it happen so I can give you a complete and accurate list."

"That's going to cost you again." Darla reached between my legs and retrieved another deeply rooted hair.

"To answer your question – and yes, I'm going to humor you for the moment – I've always had a thing for you, McCabe. So you're going to have to hop in the old Wayback Machine and think long and hard about your answer. I'll give you a couple minutes."

She leaped out of the bed and headed out of the room and back into the hall humming "Luck Be a Lady Tonight" as she left. "Be right back, baby!"

I hoped she would take her own sweet time. What did she mean, "She had always had a thing for me?" We had only met a couple weeks ago when I started looking for her brother. We were almost strangers. Applying a standard dating timeline to our time together, having dinner last night would really qualify as a first date. I had to overlook the rape; it didn't really count as a date. And then there were just the times when we seemed to run into one another unexpectedly. So, that would put us somewhere in the post-first date and pre-second date stage, and it was looking less and less likely a second date would ever happen.

I couldn't tell how long she was gone as time has a way of slowing down when you're tied to a four-poster with no hope of escape. When she returned, she had a plate, overflowing with food.

"I'm not particularly hungry," I said.

"Good, because it's not for you," she said. "This kind of thing makes me horny *and* hungry. If they could create something that satisfied both urges at the same time, I'd be a lifetime customer."

"So, back to your love life," she said, reclaiming her place next to me, enjoying some of the leftover Greek we dined on only the night before.

I recounted my entire dating history, the few times I had actually scored, the failed attempts where either they, I or my dick had fallen asleep, and the dalliances that never led anywhere for one reason or another, such as my ill-fated decision to take up with Psycho. I didn't leave anything to chance, figuring that if I left out a single person, she'd somehow know. I began to wonder who was the detective here, as she was hot on the trail of something, but what that something was I had no idea.

"Is that everyone?" she said after a time, waiting to

finish her plate before continuing the interrogation.

"As far as I know, unless you count my first kiss. Can you untie me now?"

"Tell me about your first kiss, McCabe," she said. "I'd love to hear you tell it."

Wow, I hadn't really thought about my first kiss in ages. Still, I guess no one forgets his or her first kiss. I certainly hadn't, even though it was ages ago.

"That was a long time ago," I began. "I was in fourth grade. I had this impossible crush on the girl just down the street. She was so cute, with little pigtails. She was always following me around, like she wanted to be my girlfriend. I guess today they'd call her something of a stalker."

"Pretty strong words for a little girl who was nuts about the likes of you," she interrupted. "Go easy on her. She's just a little girl in love."

"Anyway," I continued. "One day she and I were at the playground just down the street. She was totally flirting – I didn't know what flirting was back then, of course, and I don't think she did either – but I would have to say, looking back, that that's what it was.

"There we were, at the top of the slide, goading one another to see who would go first. She let go a giggle, kissed me hard on the lips and shot down the slide. When I got down to the bottom she held out her hand. I held on tight and we walked all the way home like that."

"You little slut," she said. "And what happened then?"

"Nothing," I said. "We went back to school on

Monday and acted like nothing had happened. We were just kids."

"Maybe you thought nothing happened, McCabe. "But I bet she wanted something more."

"Geez, what was her name? Debbie? Diane? Darla? It was Darla! Darla Diamoulous! How could I forget a name like that?"

"Yes, how could you?" she said, getting up to leave. Before she did, she gave me a long sip of water from a glass that was on the nightstand.

"Can I get out of the bind I'm in now," I pleaded. "Are we done with Twenty Questions yet?"

"We've only just begun, McCabe. We've only just begun."

It was 10 in the evening when I finally awoke. I had been out for hours and was still imprisoned by the power of love.

Damn. The bitch had drugged me.

Darla was nowhere to be found, but given that I could hear Dean Martin belting out Everybody Loves Somebody Sometime, I knew that she must still be here.

For the first time in my life, I felt like I was screwed. Well, I had been only the night before, but in an entirely enjoyable way, not the way I was being screwed now. Any progress I had made in loosening the ties that bind had been for naught – during my drug-induced slumber Darla had tightened everything back up again.

I wondered how this would end. Was this some

kinky game that would eventually turn into hot lovin'
or was Darla just another in a long line of psychos that I
tended to attract in life.

Worse, no one knew I was here. I didn't tell Finchley
that I was seeing Darla as I didn't want another lecture
about blending business with pleasure. I knew that it
was wrong, but I was, after all, a man and even the
most hardened guy – even a dick – wanted to be loved,
or at least lusted.

Dean was done. The record player kept up its
hypnotic click-skip, click-skip, click-skip as it waited
for someone to either start the record over or put
another on the changer.

Was this really how it was going to end? And why
would it? I thought Darla and I had something,
something that might have turned into the closest thing
I had ever had to a relationship, well, as normal as a
relationship I could possibly have.

It sure seemed that way last night. From start to
finish, it was like the best first date in history, for me at
least. But someway, somehow, the dark clouds
descended and I was now a prisoner in some crazy
game and I had no idea if I was a player, a pawn or a
prisoner.

From down the hall came a noise. Someone was still
home. I wouldn't just be left to die here from
starvation. How poetic would that be? I end up
starving to death in a house that makes King's Buffet
look as if it was managed by Gandhi.

I heard the sound of steps coming down the hall.
They weren't Darla's, unless she had put on a pair of
waffle stompers. Who knows? Given the fact that I was

tied up like a calf at a rodeo, she could be into anything.

It didn't have long to find out. The door slowly creaked its way open. And there, standing before me, was not what I expected at all.

Chapter 19

It was Darryl.

What the hell? How did this make any sense?

"Hi there, detective. Surprised to see me, eh?"

"Glad, actually. Get me out of these things. I think your sister has gone off the deep end."

"If only it were that easy, McCabe," he replied as he made his way to the corner of the bed. "This wasn't exactly the plan, but things have gotten a little complicated."

"What plan?" I said, more than a little panicked. "What is it with your family and their damned plans? You guys are starting to look a little sick."

I struggled more than ever to get free. Lord knows what Darryl was going to do. Darla seemed crazy enough, but this chicken-lickin' whack job? I really was screwed.

"It's time that you know the truth, McCabe. I didn't plan it this way, but you were getting too close, in more ways than one. So it's time we bring this chapter to a close, because if I can't have you, no one will."

Like Darryl would ever have a chance at this dick. Geesh, he was off the whack chart as well. I knew he was attracted a bit to me; that much was obvious during our brief encounter in the living room. But to imply that there could ever be something between us, something that involved two plugs and zero sockets, at least those that god made to accept plugs, was crazy talk. Unfortunately, crazy talk seemed to run in the Diamond family.

Darryl slithered into bed next to me. The stench of his last meal was still on his breath as he came closer and closer to my pinned body. I tried to find wiggle room but to no avail. He was right next to me, nuzzling in as close as he could get.

"What do you think McCabe?" he whispered. "Do you think we would have a chance?"

"Sorry, Darryl. My door doesn't swing that way. I dig chicks, not dudes."

I cried out loud, hoping someone, anyone would hear me.

"We could make this easy or hard," he said.

I didn't really like the hard option, so I played hard to get instead.

"Why don't you tell me a little bit more about yourself, Darryl?" I said. "Maybe we should break the ice with a little small talk before you decide to take the plunge."

I was hoping that would get Darryl in the mood to share his feelings instead of feasting on me, but I wasn't prepared for his opening pick up line.

"I killed them, you know. Your little girlfriends."

"So you are the murderer," I said.

"I prefer the term liberator," he replied. "Blonds are a dime a dozen and I don't really have much use for them. No one does, you know. Especially those who have a thing for my man. You see, McCabe, I've had a thing for you for a long time, longer than you could ever know. But you could just never look past my largeness to see my largesse where you're concerned."

"You have to admit, it appears to be pretty well hidden," I replied.

Darryl unbuttoned the top two buttons of his shirt. I shuttered at the coming reveal. But then I saw the necklace hanging around his neck. It was Lola's.

"That's Lola's necklace you bastard," I yelled, trying to tear free of the ties.

"I think *bitch* would be more correct," he said. For a moment, I thought he was straightening his hair but instead, he removed it. A mane of dark hair fell from underneath the wig.

"Yes, McCabe, it's me."

"Darla?"

"You fell for this just like those two bimbos did," she said. "I thought for sure you were a better detective than that. My mom told me that you had studied the photos on her mantle. Remember the photo of Darryl and I dressed up in each other's clothes? That was what originally gave me the idea to set up Darryl."

She continued to return to Darla form, removing some of the prosthetics she had applied to her face to make the transformation complete.

"Be right back, love," she said. "This stuff gets itchy after awhile."

How could I have been so stupid? Sarge had warned

me to not trust anyone, to question everyone and everything. I had been on the wrong trail all the time. Well, sort of. I thought Darryl was the Caloric Caller, not Darla as Darryl. I would have never imagined she would switch hit and become her brother.

Man, she missed her calling. She had not only mastered the look, but the voice, too. She could have made big bucks in Hollywood.

I stopped considering career options for a murderer when the awful truth came to me. I had been falling in love with the girl who killed Lola and Melissa.

Geez, why did I have such bad taste in women?

Darla returned to the room freshly showered and in more womanly attire. She still had the sapphire and diamond necklace around her neck, like a badge of honor.

"So, what did you think, McCabe? I thought you were going to piss your pants when Darryl started to make a play for you. Oh, wait. You're not wearing any pants."

"But why, Darla? Why did you kill those two innocent girls?"

"Innocent?" Darla flew into a rage. "How in the hell can you call those two bimbos innocent? They make life miserable for girls like me. All you men get hard-ons because of them but all they'll ever do is pretend to love you, then leave you high and dry. You are nothing but a brief stopover for the beautiful girls in this world, the ones God blessed with a perfect figure and in at least one case, a frighteningly large bank account. All the while we wallflowers and women of size have to fight and scrape for everything we have gotten. They won the battle before it even started, McCabe, all because they were blessed with beauty and blond roots."

"You seem to have done well, Darla," I entreated. "You have a nice house and car, the trappings of success."

"Give me a break, McCabe. I take my clothes off in front of men to make ends meet. And when I need a little extra dough, I do a little blow, or worse, let them ravage me for extra money. I'm a whore, McCabe, and it's all because of you."

"Me?" I said. "What the hell have I done?"

"You didn't love me, McCabe," she said. "I have had a terrible crush on you my entire life and you've never tried to find me, you've never looked my number up, nothin'.

"So I find you instead," she continued "And what are you doing? You're chasing the blond bimbos in short skirts all over town, never once thinking about the girl who really loved you."

"Loved me?" I replied. "You only just met me!"

I was beginning to freak out on a level I had never known before. Being spread-eagled and naked on a killer's bed can do that to a guy, even a cool private eye kind of guy like me.

"You say you remember, but you really don't, do you? Darla Diamoulous. Your first kiss? Remember? I'm Darla."

"I know you're Darla, but what does that have to do with anything?"

"Dammit, McCabe, I was that little girl you kissed. Your first kiss. I'm sure you've had hundreds of…"

"Thousands," I interjected.

"Don't make this worse than it already is, McCabe. Hundreds of kisses since, but your first kiss, it's magical. It can only happen once. And we chose each other."

"We were in fourth grade, Darla. Geez, our respective hormones hadn't even checked into the hotel of love yet. We were just two little kids for cryin' out loud."

"I know, McCabe," she said. "But inside me there's still that little girl, wanting to be loved by the little boy who took her breath away all those years ago. A guy she's never forgotten or gotten over."

"I think you're a bit off kilter," I replied.

"Off kilter?" she shot back, mockingly. "I killed two women and you're calling me off kilter? I think crazy is a far better choice, McCabe. Crazy in love with a man who barely knows I am alive!"

"But we only knew each other up until fourth grade. Then you moved away suddenly. I woke up one day and there was another family living in your house."

"My dad was reassigned to another base," she said. "He was in the military. We bounced all over the country for a while. Then he was stationed at Fort Lewis again and as luck would have it, I was transferred back into your high school.

"You didn't know it was me, of course. We had taken the Americanized version of Diamoulous – Diamond. By then my dad had been in special ops and he needed to distance himself from the family name for security reasons, or so he said. I think he was just trying to beat a payment due on an old gambling debt. You don't ditch a Greek debt easily.

"I had blossomed a bit by then. You wouldn't have even known it was me. But I knew it was you. How many Brewster McCabes are there in this world? And how many high schoolers would be quirky enough to come to school in a fedora every day? Is that the same fedora you had in high school, McCabe?"

She pointed to the one I was still wearing. At least I wasn't totally naked to the world. I still had my hat on.

"Never knew a guy who wore a hat in the sack," she said. "Anyway, you'd pass me in the halls sometimes. I could tell that you were making fun of me to your friends. As you'd pass, you'd all break out in laughter. I still had such a huge crush on you. I have to say, you were a great kisser when you were a little kid and you're much better now. Wow! Still curls my toes."

"Mine too!" I said.

"Too late for sweet talk, baby. Sorry."

She continued. "I couldn't even muster the nerve to speak to you in high school. And the fact that you were saying hurtful things about me to others made it all the worse. You tortured me, McCabe. So close, yet so out of reach. Me still loving you from afar."

"I had no idea, Darla." I said, feeling a bit ashamed at being such a shit back then. "If only I had known it was you…"

"And then what, McCabe? Happily ever after with a big, beautiful woman? You were an immature dickhead in high school. You didn't have the capacity to love someone in such a big way. We would have amused, used, then abused one another until the whole thing came crashing down in the end. I couldn't have taken the pain, McCabe. Far better to live in a life of unrequited love than to find love, live it and lose it all because neither one of you could handle that kind of love. We would have eaten one another alive."

Knowing Darla's appetite, she may have been right about that. Even now she was looking at me with those piercingly delicious eyes. I couldn't tell if she was still in love with me or just hungry.

"So why now, Darla? And why would you kill these two women?"

"Oh, I admit that I had gotten over you for a time. I went on with my life, or at least tried. After college I tried my hand at being a makeup artist, but the pay is crap. But at least I learned some valuable skills, eh McCabe?"

She let go a laugh, then on a dime, turned serious again.

"So I moved on. I took some dancing gigs and found that it was easy money. I was good with money, socking it away until I could afford a down payment on this house. Darryl was a big help back then, helping me get enough money together to afford it. For a time he roomed here, treating it like it was his house, not mine. Thankfully, he met the Canadian dreamboat and moved north.

"But he did leave some of his clothes behind in his room so he would have something to wear when he came back to the states. That made it easy to do the Parent Trap act, switching places. I'm sure he has no idea that I was the Darryl you and Detective Grist were looking for, not him. It was the perfect plan."

"Was?" I asked. "Isn't it still?"

"Not with you in the picture, McCabe. If there's one thing I've learned about you over the last few weeks is that you're still squeaky clean. You'd never get over the little fact that I iced those two bimbos. It would always come between us."

"Ya think?" I said. "I'm a former cop and a detective, you shit. You'd think I'd turn a blind eye to a double homicide? Of people I knew, no less?"

"A girl could always hope," she offered. "But now I know it will never work out. I almost feel sorry for those girls. I could have just killed you instead and be over with it."

"Kill me? But why?"

"Well," she said. "Isn't it obvious? If I can't have you then no one can."

She let go another laugh and then turned to look me in the eye with a suddenly hollow gaze.

"Idiot! You didn't choose wisely" she said. "And now you know too much. I have no choice but to kill you too."

She had me dead to rights, too. There was no way out of this. It was time to make my peace.

"How would you like it McCabe? Slow or fast? Oh, I know. Why don't I kill you like I killed them? That could be amusing."

"How did you kill them?" I asked. "I mean, after all, you're going to kill me anyway so why don't you just give me the satisfaction of knowing how since I already know the why."

"Fair enough, McCabe. It will make it all that much more interesting, at least to me. You've heard of coniine, haven't you? Good stuff. Being Greek can be a bonus when you're in the market to kill someone. I contacted my uncle back in the old country and he sent me the family recipe for hemlock. It's been in the family for ages – who do you think gave Shakespeare the idea for Hamlet? It was a Diamoulous.

"Melissa was a cinch. I got the pizza at the Italian Spaghetti House. How could anyone resist that pie? Then I drove it over as Darryl. A couple of bites and she couldn't move a muscle. Well, that's not quite true. Her eyes were as big as saucers, darting back and forth until they fell into darkness."

"And Lola?" I uttered. "What about Lola?"

"Do you really want all the gory details? Can you handle this, McCabe, in your current position?"

"You could untie me, Darla. Then I'd be in a better position."

"And let you try to turn the tables and let you kill me instead? You are a cocky son of a bitch aren't you?

"Lola took some planning, I have to say," she continued. "After she left you at the TNT that night, I followed her to the Pink Flamingo. I gave her some time to get settled in before I entered. She was making time with some Jamaican wooly mammoth. While she was distracted, I dropped a little hemlock into her drink. That took some timing, given that you just never know when the old legs would give out.

"Lucky for me, she was there just long enough. I found her in the parking lot, crumpled on the pavement next to her car, unable to move and scared to death. I had already broken the light in the lot so it would be tough to see what was going on. I quickly loaded her featherweight body into the back seat of her car, and then rifled her purse for the keys and her driver's license for the address. I brought her back to her house for safe keeping until I could figure out what to do with her after I had snuffed out her pathetic little life."

"You're killing me here," I said.

"Not yet, McCabe," she replied. "Don't be in such a damned rush."

She was killing me, a little bit at a time. That would explain why Lola's cupboards and fridge were empty. Darla had had the pleasure of a little midnight snack while she hatched her plan.

"I thought the Green Lake angle was pretty sweet," she said. "Come in by boat and no one would think twice about it and no one would ever figure it out."

"Except for the shoe," I said. "The Nike stuck in the muck."

"Really?" she said, somewhat surprised. "You found that? Maybe you're a better detective than I gave you credit for. I'll have to remember to get that shoe back when this is all said and done. Thanks for that piece of information. I didn't have time to find it myself and it was the only loose end I had. Funny how you can get in a bit of a rush when you're on a killing spree. But don't worry, McCabe, I'm going to take my sweet time with you."

"Lucky me," I shot back. "So, what's it going to be? A little hemlock cocktail for me too so that I just go numb and dumb before I pass out and expire? Is that really all you can come up with?"

"You wish, McCabe!" she said. "You really underestimate me. I thought you knew me better than that."

"I don't know you at all, you whack!" I said. You're just some dame with a screw loose who has a misplaced fixation on me."

That was probably not the right thing to say, given that I was her prisoner. Her eyes turned steely as she rose from the bed.

"Whack, huh?" she said after a long pause. "I'm the whack? I'm not the one tied up in a four-poster because I wanted to get my pee-pee wet, now am I? I wasn't the stupid one who took a pizza off of a complete stranger's hands, a pizza she didn't order, from a place that doesn't even deliver there."

She had a point. If I had kept my wits about me and my dick out of this, I wouldn't be in a such a dire predicament right now. I started to wonder how they would find me. In the thickets of the lake? Dead on the floor of my own pizza-stained floor? Slumped over in my chair in my office? This was not going to end well, but it would sell a lot of papers.

"It's time to end this, McCabe.

"To die, to sleep –
"To sleep perchance to dream – ay, there's the rub,
"For in that sleep of death what dreams may come…"

Was she trying to kill me with bad poetry?

"It's Hamlet, dolt. Figured you wouldn't understand the sweet irony that is this moment."

She shed her clothes, leaving her naked except for Lola's necklace. She climbed into the bed and straddled me.

"Really? You think I'm in the mood at this moment? Am I just a piece of meat to you?"

She didn't say a word, choosing instead to turn around, her back to me. She slowly inched her way up my torso until her butt was a mere inch from my face.

"Just so you know, McCabe. I never killed them with the Hemlock. It was just to take the fight out of them. Now you get to die just like they did."

She sat up. Her once voluptuous, enticing body now consumed all the space around my head. I was gasping for air, but there was none. What would have once been a very exciting moment for me was now one filled with shear terror. I was being butt-smothered.

I fought against the ties and the two that held my once outstretched arms suddenly came free. It wasn't my superhuman strength. It was Darla. Now in a frenzied state of excitement, she wanted to enjoy the last moments of a man's life as he struggled to free himself, his hands groping and slicing for anything he could grab hold of.

It was no use. As the life began to ebb from my body, I grabbed a ball of her long hair. She screamed out in ecstasy as the pain and thrill of killing collided in an orgasm of delight.

This was it. I was a goner.

BANG! BANG!

Darla released her death grip and fell over.

Everything was a blur as I gasped for air. Moving so quickly from the darkness of death to the bright lights of life left me dazed and confused.

As the air restored my senses, I saw two shadowy figures that slowly came into focus. It was Finchley and Grist, each shouldering their weapons as they untied my still bound legs.

"You O.K., boss?" Finchley asked.

I took a moment to consider a range of answers, all of which would begin and end with thank you.

"Yeah, I'm good," I said, still gasping for breath. "But that blood is never coming out of this fedora."

"Geez, McCabe. Really?" said Grist. "Another couple of seconds and you would have been looking down on us from above."

"I always look down on you, Grist. Even while I walk upon this earth."

He waited for me to thank him, but the moment had passed.

I pushed Darla's now lifeless body the rest of the way over and she cascaded to the floor, two bullet holes placed neatly in her forehead.

"Nice shots, guys," I said. "If I had a couple of extra large stuffed animals I'd give them to you as a prize."

I finally noticed the pain in my wrists. They were red and swollen.

"Man, those are going to leave a mark. Damn her."

I took a few moments to regain my composure and rinse the blood and other residue off my hands and arms. I also washed my face, several times, scrubbing as hard as I could, trying to clean away the memory of a sexual encounter that will undoubtedly haunt me forever.

After reclaiming my clothes, I emerged from the master bath. The detectives and coroner had arrived on the scene. No need for an aid unit. Darla wasn't going anywhere, except to a steel slab in the morgue. Her eyes were now blank, staring up at the sky, her last moments spent in a twisted ecstasy that was definitely one for the books.

I retrieved my blood and brains soaked fedora and before heading out the door, took one last look around the room that at one point had been heaven, and another a total hell. I found Grist and Finchley out on the front lawn, their faces alternatingly lit up by the flashing lights of several squad cars.

"So, how did you ever know where to find me?" I asked.

"Well, McCabe," said Grist. "I wasn't looking for you at all. It was your pal Finchley here. I just came along to see what you had gotten yourself into again."

"Why would I ever think anything different, Detective... Grits, isn't it?"

"Have your moment McCabe and call me anything

you like," Grist said. "But the boys down at the station are going to have a really belly roll when I tell them how we found you and the look on your face when Darla finally rolled off of you. I've never seen a butt-crack contorted face before. Priceless! Where's a camera when you need one?"

He smiled and walked off to his squad car.

"Thanks Finch, old pal," I said, shivering in the night air. "But really, how did you find me?"

"A bit of luck, McCabe. A bit of luck. It turns out that you parked the Monster facing the wrong way in front of the house, against traffic. Darla's cranky neighbor across the street had had enough of all her peekaboo shows and wild nights. He called the cops on the illegally parked car and the Bellevue folks, well, they're kind of picky about how people park, not like in Seattle. Anyway, they impounded your car and they called Grist to let him know that they had it because he always felt such personal satisfaction in you having yet another run of bad luck.

"Grist called the office to see where you were, largely because he wanted to rub your nose in it that he knew where your car was and you didn't.

"When he got your answering machine, he left a message, telling you that your car had been impounded in Bellevue. I picked up the message and called the impound yard and then the towing company. They gave me the location of where the Monster had been picked up. So this was the first place I checked. Good thing, too. You weren't long for this world."

"Thanks old chum," I said, putting my arm around him. "This is one time that I'm glad the Monster was impounded. She saved me again."

"Ahem. Who saved you?" Finchley replied.

"You, Finchley. You saved me."

I hopped into Finchley's car, replaying the events that had transpired over the last few days and how I almost cashed all my chips in on a night of torrid romance that turned into a horrific crime scene.

I was just glad that it wasn't me they were hauling out in the body bag. The Reaper had paid a visit on this day, in this part of town, but he left without Brewster McCabe, Ace Private Eye.

~ THE END ~

www.ingramcontent.com/pod-product-compliance
Lightning Source LLC
Chambersburg PA
CBHW030915120626
46554CB00001B/164